Five Miles from

C000259058

*by the same author*

LOVE YOUR ENEMIES

REVERSED FORECAST

SMALL HOLDINGS

HEADING INLAND

WIDE OPEN

# Five Miles from Outer Hope

## NICOLA BARKER

*faber and faber*

First published in 2000
by Faber and Faber Limited
3 Queen Square London WC1N 3AU

Typeset by Faber and Faber Limited
Printed in England by Clays Ltd, St Ives plc

A CIP record for this book
is available from the British Library

ISBN 0–571–20205–5

2 4 6 8 10 9 7 5 3 1

In loving memory of Jason, Anna and little Romy

With special thanks to Jessamy Calkin

# Five Miles from Outer Hope

It was during those boiled-dry, bile-ridden, shit-ripped, god-forsaken early-bird years of the nineteen eighties. The same summer my brother Barge started acrylic-ing his internationally celebrated collection of bad canvases featuring derelict houses with impractical tomato-red masonry and gaping windows: his agonizing L. S. Lowry period (and look what happened to *him* – a gleeful life of Northern bliss, stuck in Pendlebury with his bed-ridden mother. Pretty fucked up. Ask anybody).

And it was the identical year, more to the point, that my vicious but voluptuously creamy candle-wax-skinned sister, Christabel (Poodle for short, or Poo, if you *really* wanted to risk a trouncing) went out and invested in a brand-new pair of breasts, and then, with the kind of infuriating randomness only ever exhibited by terriers, High Church clerics, and the despicably attractive, finally got around to making the one and only decent-minded decision of her rancid, fatuous, nineteen-year-old life (a good impulse, you'll be pleased to know, that she never, *ever* recovered from).

And it was the self-same summer – June 5th, if precision is your watchword – that I first set eyes on a stringy southern hemisphere home-boy, a *man*-boy, a prankish puck by the name of La Roux (with very bad skin and even worse instincts), who sailed into the slow-beating heart of our half-arsed, high-strung, low-bred family, then casually capsized himself, but left us all drowning (now they don't teach you *that* at the Sea Scouts, do they?).

In order to pinpoint this nebulous time chronologically, to *locate* it in terms of general events of national – fuck – *galactic* significance, to set it all in perfect sync, so to speak, it was actually the very year in which that resplendent Sylph of Synth, that unapologetically greased-back, eye-linered soprano imp, Marc Almond (the rivetingly small-c'd Marc) enjoyed a late summer smash with his electro remake of Gloria Jones's old Northern Soul big-belter, 'Tainted Love', then celebrated it by devouring well over a pint of warm, pale cum in a public toilet – somewhere horribly unspecific – and got his gloriously effete wrist slapped, and his adorably flat stomach pumped for his sins.

Yes, *that* year.

And let us pause (momentarily), lest we forget the curious story of Mr Jack Henry Abbott, the bastard Yankee killer, the ingeniously literate reprobate (whose lucky-lettered surname would ensure him an opening position on the index of every World Encyclopedia of Twentieth-Century Murder for ever and ever more, amen), who in this particular summer somehow managed to prick the precious consciences of all those fine-minded, high-flying American writerly types (sure I can gloat – I lived in Texas for fifteen months. It was hot as Hades. It was dry as toast. I was resplendent in two completely random scarlet eczema mittens. I walked around with plastic bags on my hands to stop me sticking to furniture. I was medically advised not to get wet in the shower. *Medically advised*, I tell you. Call that *humane*?) and then spat, and spat again, in

4

their kindly, good-intentioned, well-bred faces. (Don't you just *love* it?)

It was that year. It was that summer. Late that summer.

It was 1981.

Remember?

So my dad loved Thurber. He had a *penchant*. What can I say? *Thurber*. The American who – so far as I can tell, anyway – made a living out of writing witty stuff on the fascinating subject of canine behaviour. And he drew cartoons of bloodhounds doing human things in a mutty way but being all high and mighty about it, like making citizen's arrests and drinking pale ale in public houses and suffering from acute depression. As if dogs have all that much to be worried about – existentially – or *superior* about, come to think of it. And this clever cheeseball made a *career* from these meanderings.

He was born in 1894 (this is Thurber, dimwit) and he lived – like my father – the first seven formative years of his life tortured by his incapacity to digest solids. Horrible gut problems. *Huge* coincidence, and hence, That Bond.

All told, there are seven of us: Big, that's Daddy. He's four foot nine in his clogs, which is pretty embarrassing, but when we were little, we were *tiny*. That's nature. We knew no better.

Painfully thin. Like a toothpick with elbows (yet in our minute consciousnesses, a giant pink radio mast, a wild, fleshy skyscraper), which is why Barge – who's already coming over slightly too idiosyncratic in these pages for my taste – went right on ahead and nicknamed him in one single syllable with his soft, slightly lisping, sweet baby-lips. *Big*.

Big does some landscape gardening. He's in the midst of

compiling a supernaturally tedious *Pocket Guide to Garden Shrubs*. He lives to crochet. He still finds it extremely difficult to digest cheese. It's a daily battle.

Okay, *Barge*. Barge! What a wit! What a prodigy! Well, the truth is this kid's name was actually lifted straight from the collar of that ridiculous ale-lapping hound I believe I might already've mentioned earlier (a mongrel, a drunk, an ineffectual guard dog – these are details only a Thurber fanatic would find telling) and he is distinguished by being the oldest child in our considerable and cosmopolitan clan. Our clutch.*

By mid-1981 Barge was living on the only kibbutz not actually inside Israel. I think it was deep in the Balkans, somewhere. He kept the faith by painting assiduously in the evenings and boiling beet for his keep. Clear-pored and righteous (This was *1981*, for God's sake. He'd never even heard Bill Wyman's 'Je Suis un Rock Star'. It was *depraved*).

Naturally the degraded root vegetable-based enclave to which he had only recently become attached consciously eschewed all unnecessary contact with modern technology. If you'd thought to ask, he'd've said *Abacab* was some kind of taxi service.

Next up, or down, was the lovely Christabel with her two brand-new, out-of-the-blue, special-purchase, proud-

---

* At the time of writing – I must debunk, for the sake of narrative accuracy – he is embroiled in that most fascinating of occupations: court illustrator, somewhere noteworthy within the salubrious confines of the great city of Woolwich. But back then, it was matchstick men, matchstalk twats, L. S. Lowry, the abandoned houses. Twenty-one years old, poor sod, and dippy as a hungry swallow – his unconscious patently embroiled in some kind of inexplicably acute trauma, his day-to-day personality far too slight and light and breezy for belief. What a *fuck* up.

upstanding, oxygen-tank tits (after she'd turned fifteen, if you called her Poo to her face, she'd string your teeth into a necklace and then make you pass it), a cheerfully malevolent teen queen, the only paid-up member of our benighted eighties familial troupe to wear normal – read as English – clothing (the rest of us stepped out boldly in our embroidered kaftans, fur-trimmed hide waistcoats and crochet knickers. We were *mutants*): I'm talking pleated skirts, high-neck blouses, court shoes. Standard hideous. All acquired – without exception – as a consequence of her devious and persistent extra-marital conjunctions.

But she was always Daddy's favourite, his pride, named after Thurber's most beloved black French poodle (although I fear close textual scrutiny reveals this animal to be an inconsistent, teasing, curly-hinded harridan: please refer to Mr T's essay on 'How to Name a Dog'. He doesn't say it, in so many words, but I believe the modern vernacular is *slut*.)

I'm next down and I'm Medve. No, it isn't a verb. And it isn't Ancient English for river or whore. Medve was also, if you must know, a Thurber canine, another poodle, not quite so beloved as Christabel, but, shucks, a great breeder by all accounts, and an independent dog blessed with the talent of throwing her own balls and then retrieving them. A bitch. Obviously.

Medve is Hungarian for bear, which, when you think about it, is pretty fucking grizzly. And don't ask me how to pronounce it. I will inflate and then I will gently burst. And it will be messy, because I am built like a shire horse. Six foot three in my crocheted stockings. I am *huge*. Sixteen years old in 1981, with a tongue taut and twisted as a tent-hook and two tremendous hands like flat meat racquets.

*Thwack!*

My serve, I think.

Sadly, I am the only recorded giant in our tribal history. There are no magnificent, monolithic, Humber-Bridge-building great-grandfathers hanging around helpfully in our fine family tree, no cousins-twice-removed making a fortune as novelty attractions in disreputable out-of-town freakshows. No one, in other words, for a poor, tall girl to look *up* to.

I am not stupid or rebellious enough to consider my difference a boon. I am anti-genetic. I am *unnatural.* And this hugeness is not even counterbalanced by any degree of sleekness or sveltness or grace. I have knees as wide as the skull of Neolithic man. They knock together sometimes, as I walk, and the subsequent crashing makes sheltering rabbits, deep in their burrows, roll their eyes skyward, embrace each other with their funny bunny arms and *quake.* I am clumsy. I *lumber.* I can only buy shoes through mail order. I disorientate seagulls.

Hang on, you're thinking (you're so transparent): *seagulls*?!

I'll get to that. Hold your horses. First off, I just want you to imagine my little mother, Mo (there's nothing cutesie in this moniker, she's Maureen, that's all), five foot two inches tall, struggling to pass my huge head through her cervix. Think small African pygmy being force-fed a planet. Mars, maybe. Or Pluto. There will be screeching. There will be retching. And tearing. And tears. Afterwards the whole Sahara desert will look like a badly managed Halal butcher's.

Poor Mo. Mo is actually very scientific. In the fifties she published her Ph.D. entitled *The Intellectual Woman's Guide to Atomic Radiation*. It was a smash. There were so many intellectual women around back then, and all of them absolutely *gag-*

8

*ging* to understand the atom. She might almost have planned it.

Naturally this fine specimen of emancipated womanhood cashed in on her little victory by choosing to spend the bulk of the following decade breeding with a man without a stomach on a series of far-flung atolls. She has a passion for atolls (not, I fear, an interest as inspiringly universal as atomics. But give it time).

By early 1981 things had picked up a little. The urge to reproduce having momentarily abated, she was fully occupied in stringing out a long-extended but very temporary American visa working alongside a rather shifty man called Bob Ranger in developing and patenting a fascinating new security device for the US prison service. An Anal Probe. (And remember, this was the kind of woman who always made a habit out of bringing her work home.)

*I don't want to talk about it.*

Well, not yet, anyway.

There are just two others; both younger and not particularly interesting. Patch. A girl. Twelve years old. Fat-cheeked. Literate. Needy. The only one among us *not* named after a Thurber pooch. Would you believe it? I mean how *harsh*. How *excluding*.

Then there's Feely (a slack, ill-bred Boston Bull Terrier), our smallest. Four. When he grows up he wants to be a bulimic (He thinks it's a veterinarian who specialises in livestock. He's so *credulous*). He's into amateur naturalism. He is obsessed by the life story of a Japanese deer called Shiro Chan, a special doe with a strange white fringe whose story Barge came across by chance once in a poor-quality Japanese travel book. It's a tragic tale. Lovely deer: road traffic accident. Oh Lord. Don't even get me started.

That's it. So I'll toss you a few crumbs, some details, to fill in, to plump out . . .

We all have bad teeth (A direct consequence of:

(a) Non-fluoridated drinking water

(b) Brushing for six years (1968–74) with only our middle fingers

(c) Never eating solids as kids.

In his mid-thirties – no doubt as a consequence of his own dreary digestive dramas – Big became really interested in nutrition and spent the bulk of the seventies developing what turned out to be an unsuccessful forerunner to the Cambridge Diet. A shake for breakfast, one for lunch. You know the story. The upshot was I didn't chew until I was ten years old. I only ever *sipped*. I suffered chronic muscle wastage in my jowls. My teeth crumbled. Everyone thought I had cheekbones, but it was only deprivation.)

And we live on an island off the coast of South Devon. In fact we've lived on a whole host of islands, bigger than this one, if you must know, and grander (Islands were the atolls of the seventies, but inverted. It's a geographical joke. Just let it wash over). New Zealand. The Philippines. Jersey. The Scillies. That shithole where they made *South Pacific*, the 1950s Technicolor army-based bikini-drama (Remember me? I was the impeccably moral girl who somehow sustained a successful military career in hair rags and prescription hotpants. Ah yes. So *lifelike*).

Guess what? Joking aside, I have no interest in geography. I'm a teenager. It's my foible. And anyway, if I stand on my tippy-toes and squint, I get to watch Margaret Thatcher crawling up Reagan's arse all the way over in Missouri. I'm a big girl. I see things coming.

In truth, the Devon thing is only very temporary: almost derelict Art Deco hotel up for sale. Needs renovating. Sounds romantic. Isn't. Big's sorting out the grounds as a favour to the current owner, who spends most of her year sucking extraneous segments of tangerine from the dregs of her sangria in a sumptuous corner of Bilbao.

And it's only part-island. When the tide goes out there's a nifty hourglass of sand attaching us, inexorably, to the remainder of the coastline. So during daylight, every six hours, the sightseers swarm over like fat ants across butter.

We live in squalor. We paint pottery for extra cash. It screws up your vision. It gives you the shakes. It's not at all cool.

But it's the summer, don't forget, and not half-bad weather, either. 1981. I believe I mentioned that already. And soon Marc's going to be at the top of the charts, all dressed in black and irresistibly nasal. And Jack Henry will publish his wonderful book, then start campaigning like crazy for early parole (just you watch as he gets it). And Dolly Parton is up on the big screen, doing it for the girls in her office-based bio-pic, *Nine-to-Five* (oh Lordy, *Lordy*, thank you, Dolly!).

And there will be riots in Brixton, and Royal marriages and the space shuttle Columbia: flying and orbiting. And somehow they'll check-mate the Yorkshire Ripper, and baseball will strike, and air traffic controllers, and McEnroe will win the US Open, and Karpov will reign as World Chess Champion, and in May, Bob Marley's short life will be over. *Cancer*.

It is the Year of the Rooster: the strangest, darkest, screwed-up time of scratching and strutting and shitting and crowing. 1981.

*Jesus Christ, my fucking ears are burning.*

# 2

*(I have pins in my ears. Flashforward, Dumbo. If my narration gets a little hot-diggedy it's because I have pins in my ears. Seven in my right, one in my left. This is acupuncture. I'm giving up smoking. And I don't even smoke yet.*

*It's very messed up. You'll find out later.)*

Let's get this straight, for starters: I *don't* have beautiful eyes. If you dare even *think* it (and I'm not kidding), then this whole damn business is over, buster. I've been knocked hard and I'm hurting, see? Because that asinine You Have Beautiful Eyes thing is exactly the kind of shudderingly clumsy gambit well-intentioned five-foot-seven morons really seem to enjoy trying out on a sixteen-year-old girl giant in mail-order shoes. So I don't want to hear it, okay?

And the truth is (more to the point), if you ever chanced to glance into the nappy of a five-month-old baby who'd recently swallowed a gallon of mashed banana on a seven-hour boat trip, well, *that* would be a fair representation of the colour of my eyes. Or if you peered into Shakin' Stevens's pituitary gland after a lengthy night out on the piss, *that* would be the colour of my eyes. I *don't* have beautiful eyes. I *do* have a beautiful chin. But unfortunately that's simply not the kind of thing people feel *comfortable* remarking upon in 1981.

It's a very dark time.

I didn't sleep much in May. *Hormones.* I'd been spending the bleached-out early hours of every morning honing my masturbatory skills with only Peter Benchley's *Jaws* (come on! Not *literally*) and Barry Manilow's 'Bermuda Triangle' for company.

My clitoris, you'll be pleased to know, is as well-defined as the rest of me. It's the approximate size of a Jersey Royal. But whenever I try and *mash* it (don't *sweat*, I know these particular potatoes are determined *boilers*, but *flow* with the analogy, for once, why don't you?), all I can think about is Mr Michael Heseltine MP eating an overripe peach on a missile silo somewhere deep in the South Downs – or the general vicinity – juice on his tie, shit on his shoes. Am I ringing a bell? Do you think this might *mean* something?

I'm still young. I don't want to develop any sick sexual habits (to plough any permanent furrows) that I may have trouble casting off later. The way I see it, sex is rather like a hair parting; if it falls a certain way, after a while, it sticks. One day, I tell myself, I'm absolutely certain I'll want to fuck Tony Hadley like all the other girls.

If, by sheer chance, you're interested in the layout, I have my portable mattress down on the ground floor in the old Peacock Lounge, next to the empty fountain with its rusty residue, the silver-tiled swoop of the cocktail bar and, best of all, glimmering high above me, the peacocked glass ceiling – every feather rattling if the wind so much as *sighs* on it – which means whenever I design to close my eyes it's like that great, big barman in the sky is mixing me a Manhattan.

Cocks aside, in those long, listless, liquid-ceilinged early hours I often find myself thinking about the big issues: Can my hair sustain a wedge? Is the Findus Crispy Pancake truly a revelation in modern cuisine? Am I 'Hooked on Classics'? Will Poodle see the folly of her ways and extricate herself from her disastrous affair with that repulsively lascivious travel agent whose skin resembles an ill-used leather hold-all? Is exploding candy truly a part of God's scheme?

Big has this great story about God which he'll tell you at the drop of a stitch if you're stupid enough to consider asking. It involves six roadkills and it explains a *lot*. Wanna hear it?

Okay. It's circa 1957, and Big is driving a group of student buddies on a wild coast-to-coast excursion through some barely roaded, shit-slicked, no-horse parts of America. Christ knows where. He is driving – this I *can* help you with, it's the question Barge always asks whenever Big cranks this story up – some old-fashioned type of American Cadillac, an ancient, dusty, sludgy green-coloured cheap rental with no air-con or heating.

It is night time. Big is tired. He is not, however, under the malign sway of any kind of boozy or druggy concoction (Patch asks this. She's interested in narcotics. When she grows up she expects to be a pharmacist. Ironically, history has much greater things in store for her; after a bumpy start she ends up being part of the team who revolutionize thermal clothing – you know, that whole pitiful nineties 'inner-wear becomes outer-wear' farrago?)

Bear in mind, this is a man with half a stomach, remember? A *dwarf*. He can barely reach the pedals without standing upright. It's not *half* so romantic as you're thinking, trust me.

Anyway, it's late. Big's pals – a group of shallow horticultural students with hayseed in their teeth and manure on their breath (this is a point of interest to Poodle, who can already identify most of Big's associates by their vasectomy scars) are dozing in the front and in the back. On the radio (this is my moment) are a selection of classy orchestral standards arranged by Glen Miller or Robert Farnon or *somebody*.

Well, Big has not been driving over-long when he sees something quick and dinky suddenly skipping in front of him. He blinks. There on the road stands a tiny fieldmouse. He brakes, quickly, but still he hears the inevitable 'ka-*ting*' and then feels the front left-hand wheel hiccup slightly. Oh *dear*.

Big drives on. Twenty minutes later, he turns a sharp corner only to see a jackrabbit standing in his headlights like some kind of out-of-work *Disney* character: up on its back legs, its little paws flailing. He can't even brake. *Phut!* Dent in the bumper the size of a turnip. Fur on the mudguard. The rabbit, I fear, is plainly no longer.

He drives on . . . Okay, I'll cut this short as I'm presuming you're a quick learner . . . Next up, a racoon. He's lucky this time – just clips it. It squeals like a banshee then jumps up and scarpers.

*Yikes!* A dog. A manky farm pooch. *Bang!* He's whacked and he's winded. Big does what he can to help the creature. Trawls it back to the farmhouse, et cetera.

Not even an hour later – you guessed it – a sheep. Swerves to avoid. Manages it. *Phew!* Then finally, the big one. A cow. Large cow, just standing in the road, licking its nose, quietly passing the time of night like its whole life has been leading to this one exquisitely meditative moment.

By this time, Big is so head-fucked that he drives off the road, into a tree, and spends the rest of the night half-way up it.

Let's get this straight. It is not the fact that Big has experienced the horror of six potential roadkills in one single evening that disturbs him (and the bottom line is, only two of these animals were squelched for sure), it's the fact that he suddenly perceives the simple truth that these night creatures were arranged into some weird kind of *order*: smallest to largest. And in his mind, this orderliness contains vague – I'm talking *really* vague (he doesn't shave his head or enter a monastery or anything) – implications of Divine Intervention.

(Let us not forget – this is Feely's contribution whenever he hears this particular story – that llamas have an inbuilt need to arrange themselves in order of size. It's just an instinct, Feely opines. Ask any llama farmer – yeah, so do you happen to *know* one? – and they will all swear blind that if you go to bed with your fields full of llamas, plodding about their business, quite arbitrarily, when you eventually awaken, the llamas will, *without fail*, have arranged themselves into an immaculate line: tallest one end, smallest the other. They will be in *perfect* order, ready for inspection. That's llamas. They are bloody obsessive.

An interesting fact, certainly, but not, I fear, particularly pertinent to the story at hand. But he's *four*. And let's not forget that whole tragically morbid Shiro Chan thing, either. Which *is* pertinent. As a matter of fact it's a rather sensitive issue. So give the little runt a *break*, will you?)

If there is a God, Big maintains, then (and this is the important part) he is surely a *very pedantic* deity. For some reason Big finds this notion a source of great comfort. Perhaps it's because he is an extremely pedantic man himself at heart, and the idea that God has seen fit to arrange the whole world in perfect sync with his own shortcomings is, quite frankly, rather flattering.

In my opinion, there are many other adjectives I'd rather associate with the Creator of All Things: muscular, avuncular, priapic, whiffy, bolshy, galvanized, funky. Pedantic, in my book, just doesn't really cut it. Sorry.

Like *you* care.

I should fill you in on the Poodle thing. And be warned, it's complicated. So I'm going to take some stuff for granted; the basic social and geographical organization of the Scilly Isles in the years 1979–81, for one thing.

If you care to imagine it (approximately fifty islands stuck slap-bang in the middle of the gulf stream), we were washed up on Bryher for eighteen months (golf course, small hotel, a scattering of sheep, high winds, too much granite. A teen dream, basically).

Big is working on Tresco in their famous gardens (even I can't knock Tresco, with its ravens and exotic flowers and shit). But all *civilized* life is happening on St Mary's, which is kind of the capital of this shredded little universe, and it is in this place that Poodle – who is making money selling T-shirts in a tourist shop – catches the eye of a physically repellent cod fisherman called Peter Bunch.

Now Poodle has had many offers. She is a very pretty lady. She has this inadvertent post-punk/pre-goth Siouxsie and the Banshees/Kim Wilde 'Kids in America' pale-skinned, back-combed hair thing going on which is pretty bloody irresistible – especially to men over forty, not least the head of St Mary's travel kingdom, a swine called Donovan Healy, who is coincidentally promising Poodle the world as her whelk if she wants it.

Mo, naturally (as any good mother would be), is sharp to his manoeuvrings, and just before setting sail for the States makes Poodle promise to look elsewhere for her *entrées*. Poodle merely sneers, which for her is pretty damn obliging.

Pete Bunch, it must be said, is only known throughout Scilly for one thing: the grandeur of his astonishing overbite. His top jaw hangs over his bottom lip like . . . go on, create an image for yourself. Preferably something to do with Venezuelan Swamp Hogs or the *Beano* . . . But if there's one thing you can't take away from him it is the undeniable fact that the man has *balls.*

He is the ugliest, stupidest, most unappetizing reprobate in all of the fifty isles (gannets included) and it is because of this, and as a matter of sheer *perversity*, that he sets his sights on my beautiful sister.

I know what you're thinking. You're thinking *surely that surly, sassy, egocentric bitch can look after herself?* And you'd probably be absolutely right, if you weren't, on this occasion, the complete and utter opposite.

I must just – as a kind of aside – let you in on one of Pete Bunch's sad little *routines*. The Italian pop star Joe Dolce (a one-man reason why joining the EC was such a huge, fucking catastrophe) was at this particular point riding high in the charts with his nightmarish novelty hit 'Shaddupa Your Face', and Pete Bunch is so tragic that he has adopted this little ditty as his trademark song of the moment and is walking around the town doing the most *pathetic* Joe Dolce impression, with hand-gestures and everything, that you – or any sentient being – have ever seen.

Naturally when Poodle first sets eyes on this (and remember, she's the girl who has travelled the whole world, carelessly feeding on its rich and remarkable multicultural bounty) she thinks it's one of the most embarrassingly *fatuous* displays she has ever, *ever* come across.

The problem is, the man is so depraved, so stupid and persistent that she almost feels *sorry* for him. And you know what that means? Her defenses come down a little (this girl *invented* defensiveness) and she starts to find him pitiful, but, well, *pitiful*.

As any sharp mind will know, it's a terribly short step from *pitiful* to go-on-then-and-fuck-me. In less than twelve days, Poodle is crammed into the cabin of a fishing boat, mid-way between Gugh and Samson, yanking her knickers down and sucking on this Dolce wannabe's obscenely protrusive upper set. It was sheer madness.

But it doesn't end there. Any intelligent person might think that Mr Bunch would be insanely gratified at the idea of casually dating the most beautiful creature then currently inhabiting the Scillies. And they would be *wrong*.

After only one piece of interaction, Bunchy goes all cold on Poodle. And while the truth is that Poodle only really ever intended their canoodle to be a one-off thing – she deserves a man with status and money, doesn't she? – she doesn't get a chance to knock The Bunch back because The Bunch knocks her back *first*, and for one very specific reason.

Every pub and bar in St Mary's is *alive* with it. Bunch won't screw the new girl again because she has no tits. He is a tit man. She has none. And that is his bottom line.

It is at this point that things get a little shaky. The titless, shitless Poodle-related gossip gets so swollen and inflated and dark and vicious that eventually Big feels obliged to step in himself and stop it. He says not a *word* to our Poodle on the matter – God *forbid*. Instead he chugs quietly over to St Marys, calls Pete Bunch out and gives him what for. Barge, naturally, is working as back-stop.

It is all very humiliating. The man is four foot nothing. Bunch laughs in his face (or the clean air above it) and poor Barge is obliged to step in and steady things. In the process, he loses the tip of his tongue, a slightly ironic injury, really, considering the fact that his tongue hitherto had always been too long and hence slightly lispy. Now it is slightly short and the net result is not – you stupid dreamer! – a miraculous cure of his former difficulty, but one of the worst speech impediments in the whole northern hemisphere: with the added bonus of a future literally *dripping* in spittle and indignity (french kissing? Out of the *picture*).

Wow.

That Pete Bunch could *really* sock it to ya.

## Epilogue

You might think Poodle would be grateful for her family's intervention in this island drama. You would be wrong to think so. She is livid. She will never forgive Barge for losing his tongue on her account. She will never forgive Big for being so small. She will never forgive Mo for buggering off to America just at the juncture when her moral guidance skills were most needed, and the whole, damn family, more to the point, for being so strange and weird and different and tall and kaftan-ridden and freakish and poor and lean and curly.

She falls, henceforward (has the girl not an *ounce* of original-ity?) into the leathery arms of Donovan Healy. He has volun-teered to ease the pressure for a while by getting Poodle off the scene in some kind of phoney, bull-shitty couriering capacity.

And that is how Poodle becomes Healy's whore. But there is a price to pay. And Poodle *won't* be paying it. She has been burned. She has been spurned. The bitch, as they say, has truly turned.

Shortly after, we stagger back to the mainland, our numbers cruelly depleted: Mo-less, Barge-less (the poor boy can't even talk for three months after, then there's the *infection*), Poodle-less. A mournful, slightly moth-eaten rag-bag of a family. Feely, Patch, Big and me.

## Appendix

She had *lovely* breasts, dammit. That's the worst part, really. Tiny chocolate-button-tipped conches, soft as a moth's wing, pale as a priest's kiss. *Lovely* breasts.

So screw that infuriatingly gormless, over-bitten, cod-fishing Peter Bunch to hell and back, I say.

# 3

I'd hate you to have me down as the world's greatest ever
L. S. Lowry fanatic – the man couldn't interest me *less* – but I
must get something off my chest about how sick and dis-
gusted I feel over the treatment doled out to this silly,
scratchy, mother-loving, messed-up art-genius in his dirty old
home town of Pendlebury.

Pendle-where? Ah, *precisely*. You see the rudimentary facts
of the matter are these: initially Lowry dwelled a life of infi-
nite contentment in Victoria Park (a smart, suburban area of
Manchester, vastly Pendlebury's social superior), before,
rather tragically, his dad's oxtail soup business went all to
seed and a move down-market became horribly obligatory.

Let us not for one *moment* pretend that it was the dream of
Lowry's life to end up living in a mill-ridden shithole with
nothing to recommend it bar a whole host of spindly cats,
rheumatic brats and cockroaches. No, sirree.

That said, the man soon set out, singlehandedly, to steam-
iron this god-forsaken buttock of a place into the annals of Art
History. No one can deny that Lowry put Pendlebury on the
map with his bad brush and his keen eyes and his soft oils. He
made it matter. He gave it *soul*. He offered it a shot in the arm
of much-needed bloody integrity.

And as he did so – records maintain – he was the absolute
living *epitome* of patience and politeness and calm, sweet

modesty. He weren't no fat-head or bully or big-gob. Quite the contrary.

(Okay, the man had some serious mental health issues. He was still a virgin aged eighty. He was chronically depressive. Wanna make something of it?)

So how do you imagine this beleaguered little area goes about *thanking* L. S. for all his crucial Northern Realist creativity?

'They laughed at me for thirty years in Pendlebury,' quoth he. To be laughed at for thirty years! L. S. Lowry. *Laughed* at by those wank-ridden tosspots in Pendlebury. Those smug, piss-infested, self-righteous, small-minded, ill bred *bastards*. Those *losers*. Those *fools*. Those *inconsequential* small town *scumbags*.

You know what? Sometimes it feels pretty damn hard for a six-foot girl giant to love the world.

(So I lied about the oxtail soup business. That's hardly the *point*, is it?)


Yes, yes, *yes*, I am a truly, irredeemably, unapologetically moo-faced, big-blotched, large-arsed, yank-my-udder Friesian (how can I deny it?), but I *do* have some inkling as to how poor old Poodle felt over the Bunch disaster. Humiliated. Small. Cast-off. Ugly. . . . And the strange thing is, I *miss* her. For a short while the sweet May sun suddenly shines just a little less brightly on our tiny, ten-acre almost-island.

Oh *please*. You actually *believe* this stuff? Jesus H! I'm so full of shit my *ears* are dripping. Miss the bitch? Are you *kidding*? I'm in my fucking *element*. It's like I've suffered for sixteen years with a dose of Bell's Palsy, and suddenly it's lifted. It's gone. I am no longer disfigured by the shadow of my nasty sibling's shallow, sulky, arse-aching misery. I mean, this girl made Ian Curtis look like Zebedee.

At last, at long last, I am free (You really expect me to mourn the brief bliss which has suddenly entered our once-dark world with all the unexpectedness of an exotic fungus sprouting on a once-putrid pile of manure? What do you *take* me for?)

I am buoyant. I can boss Patch into performing all the kitchen chores. I can mess with little Feely's head then send him straight to bed. I *rule* this damn ten-acre patch with a rod of cod.

I spend my days peering into rock-pools, fishing, swimming in the cove, snarling at tourists, flirting (pathetically) with local yokels and marching around this dilapidated Art Deco hotel like a six-foot Queen Tut in carpet slippers.

I'm still painting pottery. We're doing a concession of Thatcher mugs: mustard-yellow hair, sharp blue eyes. We are part of the zeitgeist, so why oh why do I feel so oooooh . . . *grubby*?

Come *on*. I'll get over it.


Then, out of the blue, with no prior warning, something rather peculiar happens. Over breakfast. For some reason, on the morning in question, we are partaking of our victuals in the snooker room. *Huge* table, covered in a thick sheet of protective plastic. Dark green walls, no windows, but all the vital central action carefully low-lit by a long, rectangular fluorescent strip which hangs over the table like some kind of gratuitously industrial extractor fan. It's a magical chamber; fuzzy-edged, subterranean, bruised, mysterious.

We all have our stools and sit perched upon them, miles apart from one another, like dirty-etched characters in a Rembrandt painting; half-lit in the dark-light. The room *reeks* of damp.

This is where Patch has chosen to serve. No one says anything. It is her decision. She's *twelve*. If we make too much of it she gets to think she's *interesting* or something.

I am wearing my cheap, synthetic nightdress (a garment so flammable that if I fart the buttons tinkle) and a long crocheted knee-length waistcoat. Rubber flip-flops. My heels hanging over. Hair like Medusa.

We are eating kippers with our fingers. And drinking goat's milk (Feely has a dairy allergy). It's all pretty primeval. Either way, I am finishing my first fish (telling Feely his feet are stinking), lifting up my glass, swigging on it – eyes unintentionally rolling – when *yik*! I espy a total stranger. Over the table. In the half-dark.

I stop glugging, burp, and put down my glass. He is staring at me morosely. Big, meanwhile, has quietly and most *inconveniently* abandoned the baize. Patch is telling Feely his feet stink (the girl's my fucking *echo*), and for a split second I consider how uncool it would be if I ask him straight out who he actually *is*. I don't want to be wrong-footed.

(Instantly I see he will wrong-foot me – he has that kind of jaw, and he's ginger – and don't forget I'm in my flimsy nightdress with my nipples doubtless digging like blind moles through the holes in the waistcoat crochet – why can't the man just *knit* for Chrissakes?)

'Chin,' the stranger says suddenly, and points at me. It's dark. His poky finger is lit for a second like silver. He withdraws it again, into smudginess.

25

'What?' I say, rather rudely, blinking at him. He is weird-accented.

'Chin.' He points to his own chin in the bored manner of a man much-accustomed to being misheard.

'Oh.' I wipe my hand over my chin, thinking I have milk on it, but I feel no hint of moisture.

'You have a handsome chin.' He smiles. He has an effeminate manner. His lips are thin and prone to pursing. Already I smell him; kind of clean but rotten. Bad antiseptic. Not erotic (like I'd want to shag a *drain*).

I look down. 'Can you see my nipples through my top?' I ask. He stares fixedly.

'I believe I can,' he sighs.

I nod and continue eating. The stranger stretches over, picks up a book from the place where Big was sitting previously, and then quietly starts reading it. *In the Belly of the Beast*, by Jack Henry Abbott. Hardback. Boring cover.

'Mo wrote,' Patch mutters, and tosses me a letter. I nod, pick it up, unfurl, and not another word is spoken.


Big is no help *whatsoever*. He is weeding the tennis courts when I finally catch up with him. 'So who is he?' I demand. Big straightens.

'Did you see Mo wrote?' he asks.

'Yep.'

'What did she say?'

(He loves to receive his news second-hand. And he needs to buy some reading glasses. Feely used his last pair in an outdoor experiment – he wanted to set fire to the sea – and a freak wave took them. The child is so damned ill-*bred*.)

'Deep South. Death Row. New Lawyer Friend. Some strange, fresh angle about the Probe being marketed as a means to *improve* prisoner safety and dignity (my God, the woman's such an *opportunist*). Worried about Barge's tongue. Poodle's been visiting. And the book. She sent it.'

Big nodded. 'I don't like this new prison reform stuff,' he says, passingly. (Big *loathes* progressive politics. The man's a Nazi.)

'I could give a shit,' I say.

'Watch your mouth.' He looks into the sky. A gull's flying over. Greater Black Backed. It squawks at me.

'All the same, bad Elmore Leonard novel or *what*?' I snipe.

Big just frowns.

(These are the conversations we have. They're profoundly inconclusive. But it's all that's really necessary. I won't change him. He won't change me. We're our own fucking people.)

Big bends over and picks up his weeding implement again.

'His father', he offers finally, 'is a gynaecologist. He delivered Feely in Wellington, remember? We owe him a favour. He's from Cape Town.'

'Clipped vowels. Horrible.'

'That's the nature of the beast.' Big looks uneasy. He scans the horizon.

'How long will he stay?'

Big shrugs, squats, starts truffling. Not long, I surmise, by the look of *him*. I move on.

*Hmmn.* Something tells me Mr Big is definitely not Mr Happy.

*'Don't you find being a woman in the eighties complicated?'*

*Jessica Lange*, Tootsie

Are you telling me – I said are *you* telling *me* – that it's gonna be a whole other year before that monumental short-arse Dustin Hoffman gets to set the whole world straight on the fundamental dilemmas of modern womanhood in his cross-dressing masterpiece, *Tootsie*? But where does that leave things, currently? I mean *feministically*?

Meryl Streep taking it up the arse and looking wantonly choleric in *A French Lieutenant's Woman*? Marg Thatch writ large – all nose, no jaw – in her preposterous pearls and pinstripes? Sue Ellen in *Dallas* with her pop eyes and alcoholism? Or do they honestly expect me to seek succour from that inconsequential drippy-draws playing the worthless girl part in *Chariots of Fire*? Can this really be *it*?

Look, there's not a damn thing wrong with my sexuality (excluding those private issues detailed previously), but show *me* internationally acclaimed actress Jessica Lange in

(a) grey sweatpants

(b) a nurse's uniform

and – screw Hoffman – even *I* get a little horny.

I'd better tell you about the barman. It's a touch convoluted, but bear with me. The point is (can you hear me backpedalling like fucking crazy?), when you move around a lot you get to meet plenty of new people and, frankly, you don't give a damn about them – not *really* – because in your heart of hearts you both know it doesn't really *count*, for one (you're just treading water, dammit), or *matter*, for another, however much you screw each other over, because soon you'll be gone and it'll all just be water under the hump-backed proverbial.

(You're calling my family a bunch of *users*? Spot on. You're sharper than you look. We prefer to call the whole sordid fly-by-night exchange thing 'a short-cut to intimacy'. *Ha!* God fucked up good when he gave *us* vocabulary.)

There's this small pub on the island: the Pilchard Inn – the pilchard used to swim these waters, way back, but now the Gulf Stream has shifted and they've taken to foaming further afield; they're canny. It's three hundred years old. Balanced precariously half-way up the one and only pot-holed, sharp-tilted road which staggers dejectedly from the beach to the hotel.

Mud-coloured inside, with big fish jaws on the walls and stuffed birds. Smells of dust and treacle. The owner's nephew still runs it. Keeps it ticking over. Twenty-five. A tragic soak. Stinks like brandy and dry-roasted nuts. Huge, brown eyes (a thyroid problem, but let's not spoil it). A dark heart. They call him Black Jack. Like the card game (I've never played it).

Barely speaks a word. Caters to the tourists. Resents our presence like a rat resents Rentokil. He is literally *filthy*. Naturally I have it in mind to seduce him. Or for him to seduce me. Come *on*, the man's a modern Heathcliff with his catatonic dial, his cat-gut breath, his loose, lardy belly (So I'm only four inches taller. I picture it as an act of revenge, on his part. Well *hell*. Beggars can't be choosers).

In the absence of all other island staff, Jack has been temporarily placed in charge of the Sea Tractor – a mythological machine in these parts: half bird, half monster, which, when the tide is high and the conditions are tolerable, we use to ferry post and people and provisions one way and another.

It is his pride. Seven-foot-wide wheels attached to twelve-foot-tall stilts. On top, a kind of oily, open-sided tram carriage. It chugs through the water like a superannuated steamroller.

I have cunningly been employing monosyllabic Jack's passion for this vehicle in my four-pronged attack on his affections. Last week I cleaned it. This week I'm expressing an interest in its rudimentary mechanics. I've invited him out fishing (I'm a dab-hand, me). And all the while I bore him with tales of our time on Soames Island in Wellington harbour, New Zealand. He *loves* it.

(Jack has this fantasy about turning our current crummy bolt-hole into some kind of nature reserve. He's a nutter. He likes to mutter about the surf and stuff. He's into Polynesian culture. He even has a Maori tattoo.

The man is plainly out of his tree. I mean, how does he plan to keep nature reserved on a place part-connected to the mainland? In truth he's nothing more than a tragic booze casualty, but somehow, in some way, he brings out the nasty, sexy, six-foot Nurse Nightingale in me.)

This particular morning I find him standing on an overturned bucket, poking his nose into the ancient inn's low-slung but very clogged-up gutters. It's still high tide. We're cut off. The coast is clear. And luckily my extra inches mean I don't have to yell up at him.

'Need a hand?' I whisper.

He jumps and scowls. 'Why did God make *you* so obliging?'

Side-on he looks like Gene Wilder. But no perm. I say nothing. (What do *I* know of God's intentions?) Instead I peer through a window then saunter down the hill a way.

'So who's the freak in the balaclava?' he asks. He can't help himself. He *wants* me. I stop sauntering.

'Balaclava?'

'Five this morning, I brought him over on the tractor. Your dad was spitting fucking *tacks*.'

I shrug. I am mesmerized by the sheer sum of words spilling out of him.

'Sorry,' I finally manage again, 'you said *balaclava*?'

'Then not ten minutes since,' he continues, 'I saw him carrying a shitload of chicken wire . . .'

He points to the hazy summit – past the old croquet lawn, towards the Herring Cove – a sumptuous grass-strewn rise glimmering with an obscene verdancy in the early summer shine (the cliffs crash beyond it, all chalk and shag).

'That way.'

Jesus, the man is almost *trippy*.

He peers again, 'And there he goes . . .'

I walk back towards him, up the hill. Once I reach his level I stretch my neck. Sure enough, I see a black-headed creature processing regally along the horizon, arms full of silver.

'Chicken wire? Where'd he get that from?'

'And he's got some old lavender,' Jack observes almost squinting, 'and a fucking tonne of blue grass . . . Still in his balaclava, note. The *twat*.'


You know what? He's been here all of three hours or something and already the bastard's *appropriating*. He's *re-inventing*. He's running bloody riot. Collecting chicken wire for no known reason, and gathering lavender. Wearing a *balaclava*.

Oh, so he's softened you already with the chin thing, has he? You think I didn't notice? You have a *handsome* chin. You think that didn't *impact*? This man is clever, certainly. But I am single-minded, oestrogen-fuelled and *cunning*.

Right. So he sees me coming from way off and is courteous enough to stand waiting. As I draw closer – I am panting a little and wet-legged from the dew (I'm resolutely bare-footed – my soles are like emery boards. You can strike matches off them. We do it all the time in winter), I see that the balaclava has no nose or mouth holes, although the wool's much darker where the mouth and nose should be. Wet. Sweaty.

'And the chicken wire?'

He stares at me, hazel-eyed. My words hang in the air a while. Soon they're flapping like old underwear on a windy washing line.

*And the chicken wire?*

He blinks.

'Oh. Was that a question you just asked me?'

(Imagine his words, all tight and clipped and southern hemispherical, but completely ensnared by woollen weave – *Uh. Gnah, gnah, gnah, gnah, gnah, gnah, gnah, gnah hi*?)

'Sorry,' I lie. 'I cannot understand what you're saying through your mouth.'

He still looks quizzical.

'Sorry,' he answers eventually, 'I cannot hear what you're saying through my ears.'

He proffers me the bunch of blue grass. I stare at it, impassively.

'Are you offering that grass to me?'

He nods.

'And the chicken wire?'

'No. That's mine. I have need of it.'

I take the grass. He grunts his satisfaction at our transaction then strolls away.

'Thank you,' I finally yell, but he's already twelve steps down the hill. I inspect the bunch then look up.

Four foot off, perched on the clifftops, two jackdaws are quietly watching. Heads cocked, beaks glinting. I tickle my nose self-consciously with the grass's silver, whispy flower-heads, my eyes still fixed upon them.

Suddenly they lift and plummet, peeling like bells. I stiffen. Perhaps I'm paranoid, but I honestly get the impression they might be *laughing* at me. I drop the grass that very instant (well, *almost* immediately), and calmly kick it over the cliff and down and down and down, into the sea.

The mean-beaked, dirty-vented, scraggy-feathered *sods*.

# 4

I corner Patch in the Ganges Room. She likes to hang out there sometimes with Feely. It's actually the front half of an old ship (the *Ganges*, circa 1821, you *nerd*), the captain's cabin, to be precise, but sawed off and just kind of tacked on to the hotel dining-room, with a steering-wheel (not period) dug into the dark timber floor, and portholes and old wooden benches and ancient photos on the walls and everything. A view out to sea.

Patch props Feely on a box and he steers. She stands right beside him, daydreaming. I creep up behind them, minutely galled by their gentle companionability.

'Where's he taking you?' I whisper, over her shoulder.

Patch jumps from her deep reverie. '*What?*' she almost pants.

'Tobago,' Feely answers curtly.

'And then what? Swordplay? Pillaging? Piracy?'

He turns and gives me a serious look. 'You're making too much of things,' he says gently. 'It's only imaginary.'

(Who the hell made this child so *snotty*?)

Patch sniggers and Feely steers onward, rather smugly.

After a canny minute's silence (as if in quiet tribute to Feely's considerable skills as navigator and helmsman), I clear my throat, then let the little shit have it. 'This isn't Tobago, you dunce,' I pronounce firmly. 'It's Newfoundland. What the *heck* is *up* with your geography?'

'Geography?' He echoes, blinking repeatedly. I have entered his world.

'It's Newfoundland!' I repeat, then gasp, as if only now fully comprehending the shimmering blue-green vista which unfolds right before me.

Feely shakes his head. He's seeing orange skies and sandy shores and parrots in flocks and pine trees. 'It's Tobago.'

'Nope.'

'It's Tobago.'

'Nope.'

'It's *Tobago.*'

'Whatever you say.'

He pauses. He turns.

'It's *Tobago*!'

I smile pityingly, 'Of *course* it is, Feely.'

He jumps from the box, his face stricken. 'It's *Tobago*!'

'Whatever you think, little man.'

(Little man is, of course, the final blow.)

He runs off, screaming.

Proud at having done my sisterly duty, I kick the box aside, grab the wheel and steer Patch and me straight into the heart of the tropics.

'Ah, Tobago!' I croon.

(Ever seen it? Me neither.)

Patch has sat down, meanwhile, on a bench beneath a porthole and is gnawing at her thumbnail. She clearly has much on her twelve-year-old mind.

I glance over. 'You look exceptionally porcine,' I inform her.

'I hate you,' she answers cheerfully. She doesn't exactly know what porcine means. But she's probably in the area.

She's a bright kid. Reads far more than is properly healthy.

'You hate my hormones, not me,' I enlighten her, 'and in one year's time, you too will be a monster.'

'Balls.'

I let go of the wheel and slither over.

'So tell me all about the new man,' I whisper. 'The *interloper*.'

She shrugs. She's not having any of it.

'Jack says when he arrived this morning Big was *spitting fucking tacks*. I quote directly.'

Patch wriggles her toes. 'I don't know about that,' she says, then pauses, 'but I do know . . .' (The child wants my tall teen approval so *desperately*) '. . . that he's bedding down way up on the top floor. And when Big showed him a room, he double-checked the cupboard space, but insisted there wasn't *sufficient reach*, so strode next door and claimed the neighbouring suite instead. The big one at the end with the hole in the roof.'

I'm impressed. 'The man is saucy.'

'Yes.'

'Has he much baggage?'

'Psychologically, perhaps – I mean he's a *white* South African – but *literally*, none. A tiny suitcase and a very small guitar.'

(This chubby pup is facetious beyond belief.)

'Was he wearing the balaclava?'

'Initially.'

'Any reason given as to why?'

'None.'

I mull a while. 'And did he mention his name?'

Patch shrugs, 'I didn't catch it. Something stupid. French-sounding. Double-barrelled.'

'How curious.'

'Yup.'

'You have served me well,' I wave my arm regally, 'and now you may go to find and comfort Feely.'

Patch wipes her nose on the hem of her kaftan (it's hayfever season), pulls herself to her feet, then trundles away. She pauses, though, for an instant, in the doorway.

'He stole the book Mo sent us,' she informs me, 'and I want it back. Will you ask him?'


Too obvious, you're thinking? *Obvious? Me?*

Forty-five seconds, thirty stairs, two landings, one long, leaky hallway later, I lift my fist and rap on his door. The paint is peeling. It's aquamarine. Through the cracks filter the mysterious sounds of *scratching* and heaving. Some heavy breathing. Metallic jangling.

I knock again. After two whole seconds the door is wrenched open and The Balaclavaed One beholds me. He is panting like a Dobermann trapped in a summer car.

'Now what?'

(How *welcoming*.)

'I heard you scratching.'

'So?'

'Like some old *hen*.'

He pauses for a moment, as if deep in thought, then rips his balaclava off. 'I love the way,' he announces passionately (his eyebrows all skewwhiff, his hair on end with static electricity), 'I *love* the way you *think* hens have wings for arms, but when you watch them – I mean, *properly* – they actually have arms for legs.'

My face remains blank.

'I love that,' he sighs, '*dearly*.'

He rubs his two hands on his face, repeatedly, like he's scrubbing at it, and makes a gurgling noise through his mouth meanwhile, like he's standing under a waterfall. After a short-ish duration he stops what he's doing and stares at me.

'Do you have to quack to get through doors?'

I weigh him up. Ten stone. Approximately five foot nine.

'Sorry,' he chuckles, 'I meant to say *duck*.'

'Apparently you have a double-barrelled name,' I titter. 'Something silly. French-sounding.'

'Confirmed, lady.'

He straightens majestically. 'They call me La Roux.'

'How old are you?'

'Nineteen years.'

'I'm sixteen. And don't call me lady. Everyone thinks you're a freak already. That kind of formality won't improve matters.'

'Who's *everyone*? You and your little fat sister?'

'And my brother, Feely.'

'The *four* year old?'

(Already I'm regretting this tack but still I say *yes*, defiantly.)

He ponders this for a minute. 'Hmmmn. Feely too, you say?'

I nod.

'Now you've got me scared *literally shitless*.'

He gurns preposterously.

'And the man who brought you over. Black Jack. He agrees.'

'A retard.'

'La Roux,' I murmur spikily, 'the *cream*.'

'No,' he primps, 'the *mixture*.'

I give this translation a moment's thought, then sniff.

'Can I come in?'

He steps back. 'Go ahead.'

'Presumably' – I bend my knees slightly to facilitate my easy access (he almost sniggers) and walk past, glancing up at the ceiling – 'you know there's a hole in the roof?'

'I do. Your tiny father told me.'

'And there was apparently some kind of a dispute over cupboard space?'

'It's always a factor, comfort-wise, I find.'

'And how long are you intending to stay?'

As I speak I stroll through to the sitting-room. To my left, the door which leads into the walk-in storage cupboard stands tantalizingly ajar. I pull it wider. Inside lies the chicken wire, some twigs and lavender, formed into a rough oval, about four foot in diameter, dipped in the middle. In its centre is a beautifully embroidered cushion cover, a photograph of a dog, a wooden pipe, a very small guitar, some cigarettes, two odd socks, the book Mo sent and a peacock feather.

I turn, stare at him quizzically, take one step back and point.

He shrugs. 'A nest.'

'A *nest*?'

He nods. 'Indeed so.'

'Are you *broody*? Is that it?'

He just smiles.

I bend over and grab the book. 'Patch wants this back. Do you mind?'

'Not at all.'

I turn to go. He clears his throat. 'And you said your name was?'

I pause. Now he's got me.

'Medve.'

'Ah,' he smiles disingenuously. 'German for pretty chin?'

'No,' I glower, 'Hungarian for bear.'

He embraces himself and smirks. 'How *cuddly*.'

I merely growl, slap the hardback against the flat of my paw, then leave, red-cheeked and fuzzy, knowing (oh, *screw* the bugger) that this spotty, flimsy, mean-vowelled little man has pricked and pinched and skidaddled me.

# 5

Stuff your faxes up your jaxies. Terminate your damn tele-grams. Eradicate your e-mails. I just don't *want* them. Because I know, I said, I *know* that Mr James Thurber is a Full-blown American Literary Legend and that the dog business (the car-toons, the anecdotes, all the rest of that tripe) was simply an aside, a side-line, an adjunct to his other, far greater, literary masterworks. I *know* that stuff. So please, please, please just *give over*, will ya?

Anyway, facts are facts, and a patently undeniable one is that James Thurber loved his pet poodle Christabel with a *passion* (and who the hell am *I* to deny the intensity of Thurber's feelings one way or another . . .?), but (oh, here goes), if you ask me, there was one dog, and one dog alone, which the great man loved – I mean, *really* loved – way and above all of the others.

It was his very first dog, a mutt called (ahem) Rex, an Amer-ican Pit Bull, a cat-killer *extraordinaire* (I quote: 'He killed cats, that is true, but quickly and neatly and without any especial malice') and a pretty bloody *phenomenal* jumper.

When he was a kid, Thurber and his two co-Rex-owning brothers had this special sadistic little trick they'd play on him involving a ten-foot pole and a four-foot-wide garden gate.

Rex loved to retrieve. It was practically his *nature*. And he was as keen as mustard. And he was no genius, either (as is very often the way with that special, crazy, monomaniacally yappy breed of dog, the terrier).

And so it was for these three simple reasons that Thurber and his two demonic brothers engineered a game whereby the ten-foot pole was thrown *beyond* the gate and Rex was then sent to bring it right on back to them at something approximating a full-blown, smoking-paw-provoking canter.

So off Rex leaps, stumpy tail held high, mouth gaping, fully intending to retrieve that pole. He scampers through the gate, he runs straight for it, he locates it, he turns, he grips, he lifts, he gallops back to the gate again (meanwhile, his three mischievous owners, just beyond it, are calling and yelling and whistling: all in all whipping up a *storm* of general approbation) when *bam!!* That long horizontal stick hits the sturdy wall on either side of poor Rex's avowedly muscular dog shoulders, and the poor, silly, short-sighted, over-enthusiastic barker is left toothless and numb-lipped and juddering.

What a prank! What a *wheeze*! What a jaw-breaker!

There's a moral here somewhere. I hope you can find it. I have it down pat as being something to do with the touching but nonetheless naïve and irritating (to say nothing of *painful*) perils of over-enthusiasm: a kind of canine Look Before You Leap.

We use the works of Thurber, in our house (I don't know what you do with Thurber in yours, couldn't care less, to tell the truth) as a kind of pseudo-moral manual. We forsook the Judaeo-Christian tradition back in 1974 when Barge got angry with God for treating Job so shoddily (I mean, to *plague* him with boils and locusts simply for being a basically good-intentioned, well-adjusted kind of guy? Is that *fair*? Is that *reasonable*?).

Barge always felt God was a fraction too needy. If God was your brother, he'd say (or your lover, for that matter), you'd steal his specs and lock him in the cellar. We told him God would (in all probability) have twenty-twenty vision, but Barge felt God would wear glasses on account of him spending so much time – pre-Genesis, before he moulded the sun and moon and everything – struggling to read dear Thurber's wonderfully inclusive dog stories in very poor light.

We've all been there.

I *digress*.

A major 1981 early summer dilemma amongst our little island clan (Poodle aside, and the tongue of Barge, and the kibbutz and the Lowry, and the anal probe and all of that other assorted malarkey) is that during Mo's infuriatingly indeterminate absence I have been placed solely in charge of young Feely's moral and ethical development (To trust Big in this arena would be *beyond* a miscalculation, it would be downright insanity – the man's idea of house-training a puppy would be to ram a cork up its arse. He has the patience of a *mink*).

But under my careful (if intellectually fickle) tutelage the kid has recently turned morbid. Are children like bananas? When they get a little bruised on the outside, does it mean they're bad for good? To the *centre*?

Feely's propensity to empathize with inappropriate tales of animal tragedy has become a source of recent concern to me. A case in point being the intensity of his interest in the Death Of Ginger (Black Beauty's slightly snappy chestnut chum. Remember her?) as written by nineteenth-century spinster-come-Quaker-come-horse-lover Anna Sewell (a woman whose life was not just scarred but *wrecked* by an arbitrary ankle injury mysteriously sustained on a trip home from school circa 1835. Well, I *ask* you).

This is a woman – coincidentally – whose mother liked nothing better than to spend her evenings holding temperance meetings, while her father took up his marvellous vocation as – uh-*oh*! – a *brewer*. It's little wonder Anna got all her kicks talking to equines.

At first, Feely simply liked you to *read* him the segment (chapter 40, if you want to immerse yourself completely) appropriately entitled 'Poor Ginger' (to summarize: after a shaky start in life, the chestnut mare, Ginger – apparently so named because of her propensity to snap – is taken on by the squire at Birtwick Park and treated with great kindness and cordiality until she learns to open her heart and love again. Alas, certain disasters follow – remember the *fire in the barn*?! – and both Beauty and Ginger are sold on. Beauty suffers adversity with a certain degree of stoic nobility. But what of Ginger? Little is heard of her until the fortieth chapter, and nothing, I'm afraid, is heard thereafter).

Initially Feely derived large portions of – what to call it? Delight? Cheer? – *pleasure* from his companion's reading and re-reading of the Death Of Ginger (the lines 'Men are strongest, and if they are cruel and have no feeling, there is nothing we can do but bear it, bear it on and on to the end' and the slightly later 'the lifeless tongue was slowly dripping with blood; and the sunken eyes! but I can't speak of them, the sight was too dreadful' seeming to bring him especial succour).

Soon, however, a mere reading was no longer enough to

satisfy him and a certain amount of 'acting out' became necessary. Initially – this'll fascinate the psychologists among you, amateur and otherwise – Feely enjoyed playing at being Black Beauty, apprehending and then dutifully mourning Ginger's unseemly demise with an impressive degree of muscular restraint.

But after a while, his priorities changed and gradually he began to want to *inhabit* Ginger.

Henceforth, he would trot around bearing his ill-treatment and his painfully swollen joints and his cruelly injured mouth with such *piety* and *restraint* and (how to say it?), uh . . . *sanctity*, that eventually the whole farce looked in danger of leaving the realms of horse fiction and entering the exalted sphere of morbidly masochistic sacrilegiosity.

Enough is enough. When Feely began imposing 'little moments of Ginger' on his day-to-day activities (a certain tremble in the knee on afternoon walks; bolting, randomly, on fishing trips; struggling to eat his meals because of his bit-induced lower-lip deformity), Big decided he'd had it with the bastard chestnut mare, and *Black Beauty* was closed for good and placed up on a high shelf, out of harm's way.

But the boy is canny. He has found ways of sublimating his need for Ginger into other stories. And now, even (God forbid), into his readings of *Thurber* (has the child not a smidgen of dignity?), principally – although not exclusively – into the story of the aforementioned Rex, the most exalted and beloved dog of *all*.

Say, for example, I am reading little Feely the tale of Rex and the ten-foot pole (an essential moral lesson for any unapologetically attention-grabbing four year old, as I'm sure

45

you'll agree), the boy will listen keenly, he'll *seem* to be all ears, but his eyes will be travelling down the page, ever further, in the hope of reaching the end of this useful story – Rex's tragically premature demise.

And it's a nasty one. Beaten to a pulp by another dog's angry owner, Rex (only ten years old) staggers back to Maison Thurber and prepares to die. But *wait*! Two brothers are home, but where's the third? Surely Rex cannot meet his maker without first having bade a touching farewell to this kind and loving third brother?

So he waits. He fights death. He battles against it with all the final, paltry remnants of his considerable doggy will, until, at *last*, a full *hour* later: that familiar creak of the gate! That gentle step! That whistle! The third brother returns, Rex takes a few haltering steps towards him, caresses his hand with his bloodied muzzle. And then . . . and then . . .

Oh, come *on*. Talk about *milking* the bugger. Feely (naturally he's a sharp young tyke) always wants to know whether Thurber loved Rex because he died so painfully, or because he was a fighter, a cat-killer, a butt, a fool? I explain that it was because Rex was an American Pit Bull Terrier (an exalted breed) and because he was their first dog *ever*.

The first, I tell him, is always the sweetest. The first word. The first step. The first kiss. The first punch. The first pie. The first high. The first, I tell him, is *always* the best. I mean, who remembers seconds?

I don't really know if Feely finds this theory plausible. Secretly I think he still believes James Thurber loved Christabel most dearly and that Rex was only really fondly remembered for his astonishingly moving deathbed loyalty.

Sometimes, in the morning, when he's slightly late rising and I go in to wake him, I find Feely propped up on his pillows, eyes closed, mouth agape, in a perfect physical recreation of Jacques-Louis David's wonderful painting, *The Assassination of Marat* (Marat? You *know*. The crazy, messed-up, fuck-off French revolutionary). I keep telling him (when he finally stirs) that Marat died in the bath, not in the bed. Luckily, Feely fears enamel and much prefers foam and feathers. He *knows* on which side his bread is buttered.

Imagine my surprise, then (to say nothing of my horror), when I enter the hotel foyer just before three that self-same day to find the unbelievably bumptious newcomer La Roux (wearing an extraordinary khaki-coloured boiler suit with a thick brown leather belt pulled ridiculously high and tight at his waist) lounging against the dusty jet-and-mirror-encrusted reception desk, declaiming boldly from the severely banned text of *Black Beauty*, with little Feely huddled up next to him on a bean bag (Feely drags his bean bag wherever he goes; it is small and stained and purple, full of polystyrene bobbles), listening intently, his wide eyes brimming, his dirty hands entwined, his tiny, pointed chin digging into his knees.

How do I react? Calmly and with guile, that's how. I yell three simple syllables across the foyer (*Pomfret cake!*) and march resolutely towards the downstairs kitchens. Twenty seconds later I hear a gentle pitter-patter just behind me. Feely, on my trail, his bare feet hitting the red-polished concrete with all the enthusiastic slap of the small, rare but gregarious blue penguin's flippers.

47

When we reach our destination, I lift him on to a stool and retrieve the liquorice bounty from its hidey-hole. I give him one petite cake and remove a second. 'Stay here,' I tell him, 'and when I return I'll give you the other.'

At first he's mistrustful. When he was three, Barge made the same kind of promise, then didn't return for a full five hours (so he *forgot*; is it a crime?) and Mo later found Feely – all hunched-up and foetal – in the midst of sustaining a serious bladder injury. Since this time he's been a tad more cynical – the boy has *total* recall; he's like a High Court judge with a grudge – and so, as he wraps his delighted tongue around his dark prize, he asks, 'Just how long will you be, exactly? For the record?'

'Five minutes at best.'

He nods, sucks ferociously, kicks his feet and stares up at the ceiling, two tenacious rivulets of snot trickling from his nostrils like a couple of keen, green maggots making good their escape from a flesh-toned apple.

When I arrive back upstairs, La Roux is still lounging against the counter casually turning the pages on Anna Sewell's equine homily. He glances up briefly as I enter. 'Let's face it,' he mutters, 'this book amounts to little more than a half-witted piece of flapdoodle.'

*Flapdoodle?*

'Fuck you,' I say. 'It's a classic.'

He continues paging. 'I mean, how could one woman ever make so much *fuss* about a stupid small-scale ankle injury?'

'Did *you* ever injure your ankle?' I ask defiantly.

'Twice. I sprained my left ankle in 1976 and then broke the same leg four years later in a terrible rabbit-hole calamity.' He pauses, then calculates. '1980. Last year. What is a Pomfret cake, anyway?'

Since I don't reply immediately, he glances up again. Unfortunately I have become momentarily distracted by the sight of his genitalia in his preposterously high-yanked boiler suit, where they hang on his left thigh, all limp and lopsided, like a small bag of crushed intestines newly liberated from the back-end of a turkey.

Three seconds too late and blushing slightly, I open my hand to reveal its foul black bounty. The Pomfret cake.

'Not so much a cake', I explain, 'as an edible instrument of torture.'

He leans forward, frowning. 'I can't see.'

I step closer.

'Show me properly.'

I draw closer still. Soon we are only two feet apart. He peers into my palm, intently. I peer too, sensing his bad skin, smelling its antisepticness. And I'm just about to explain how they taste disgusting, like tobacco, and about Feely's dairy allergy, and the fact that after sucking his mouth turns brown and how he likes nothing better than to stare at it in the mirror, when, in a flash, La Roux's left arm snakes out (with all the sudden velocity of a viciously pale-skinned, striking cobra), grabs a tight grip of *my* other arm, pulls it towards him and thrusts my hand, palm-upwards, into his high-held, soft-centred and utterly reprehensible gizzards.

The Pomfret cake arches skywards, I gasp and topple, La Roux bellows victoriously, fully cognisant of having humiliated me *comprehensively* (I suspect this man might still have some outstanding issues remaining with his mother. I mean,

49

who *was* this woman? A modern-day vixen with the con-
flicted soul of Lucretia Borgia?)

So, *lummie*, what's a girl to do under such trying circumstances but to grab and twist and squeeze for all she's worth?
(I have hands with a grip like Goliath's from kneading bread
and extracting carrot, celery and beet juice *daily*.)

*Ha.* Now the jack-boot's on the other foot! La Roux's fleeting but nonetheless *nasty* little grin of victory soon transmo-
grifies into a violent squawk of downright displeasure. And
when he's sufficiently displeased – which is *pretty bloody* displeased – I relinquish my grip and then run, hell-for-leather.

A childish impulse, I know. It's kind of a brother/sister
thing. He's older and meaner, but – thank the Lord for tall
mercies – I'm a damn sight bigger.

That said, what a complete and utter *bastard*, don't you reckon?

# 6

I stumble across that good-for-nothing, pre-pubescent Patch, huddled snugly into a soft, grassy dip on our most westerly clifftop, all cross-legged and pink-cheeked and wind-thrashed, gazing down and out into the grey-blue grandeur of Bigbury Bay, clutching the book Mo sent tight to her chest and meditating deeply.

Get *this*: way before I even get a *chance* to reprimand her sharply and fully and roundly for her sudden, shameless abandonment of snotty little Feely (I've dragged him along with me – he currently has his left hand stuck tight inside a plastic mug with a terrible, half-worn illustration of what looks like Mickey Mouse fellating Pluto on the front of it), she expansively casts out her chubby arm, points to the green-humped horizon behind her: the distant white-daisy-headed settlements dotting the spine of this chalk-chiselled coastline, and asks in a voice *impossibly* breathless and chimerical, 'Medve, do you think you might tell me . . .' I mean, the girl's literally *gasping*. It's so ludicrously *Jackie* '. . . the real difference between Inner and Outer Hope?'

'Of *course* I can,' I bridle, squinting with sour-eyed sisterly efficiency. 'Outer Hope is apparently much bigger. It's in bold print on the map, which I imagine must count for something. I'd guess it's approximately five miles down the coast. A small town, possibly. Inner Hope isn't in bold and it's a short distance further. At best a village. At worst, a hamlet.'

(So *what* if I said I didn't like geography? This is Medve The Older Sister at work: a role which never fails to bring out the apprentice girl Fascist in me.)

She shakes her head. 'That's not what I mean at *all*. It's not a geographical question. It's kind of . . .' she pauses, '*metaphysical*.'

Not *geographical*? I squat down in front of her, enraged by this unexpected surge of youthful precocity. 'You're *twelve years old*!' I bellow. 'What need have *you* of metaphysicals? Get back indoors, you chubby, godforsaken little whore and play with your fucking *Barbie* like every other ill-adjusted puppy-fat-ridden girl your age.'

I toss Feely towards her. As he tumbles he taps himself on the head with his mug-covered paw and gives a slight bleat. His tongue is the colour of diarrhoea. Patch catches him deftly and plumps him onto her capacious knee. 'I *knew* you wouldn't get it,' she murmurs, then inhales deeply and stares out towards the horizon. The girl's so smug, so self-important, so *mumsy*.

I stand and turn.

'*You gangly bitch.*'

I turn back again. 'Did I hear you mutter something, or was it just the gulls spewing at the sickening bulge of your second stomach?'

Feely, who *of course* takes his translating responsibilities very seriously, serves, temporarily, as a most-minor adjudicator. 'She said *You gangly bitch*,' he repeats, his emphasis all up the creek, as if he's speaking Hindi or Urdu or Pekinese. Then he pauses and shakes his cup-hand thoughtfully, 'Whatever the heck *that* means.'

Ah. The *innocence*.

Patch, meanwhile – just check her *out*! – is rubbing the grass stains off her knees, whispering something wholly reprehensible into little Feely's ear and smiling like Buddha. The *brat*.

In our house (okay, in our *hotel*, you anal blighter), we never ever eat a proper dinner. We graze. We wander hither and thither, like Thompson gazelles, or dik-dik, just plucking and nibbling. We pick and mix. It's kind of a low-maintenance familial buffet.

Big's totally *against* proper dinners. On his list of priorities, the debunking of the very *notion* of a proper dinner comes extremely high indeed – just below an aversion to bestiality (although if feelings are mutual, he certainly might waver) and casual infanticide. In Big's mind, The Proper Dinner is like a slap in the face to your bowel. It's a digestive Pearl Harbor.

So our evenings are all rice cakes (Big imports them in bulk from the US – where apparently they don't turn a hair at the concept of food-as-polystyrene – they're so well *up* on healthy living), green olives, hummous and sugar-free peanut butter. For pudding: dried apricots and prunes reconstituted in warm water. No sweetening. Evaporated milk, if you're lucky. Fennel tea (*great* for the gut). Elderberry compress for the under-sevens.

Big loves Japanese fare, but only the stuff you can boil for five hours on the understanding that it'll *promise blind* to hold its shape and remain tasteless, bright white and viscous. He's into seaweed. Squid and wholemeal noodles. But only on feast days and weddings. Followed by ritual purging and emetic cleansing. Of course.

I know for a fact he thinks soy sauce is a Chinese conspiracy to keep communism unhealthy. And ketchup or HP? The *Devil's linctus*. I mean did one man *ever* spend so much time considering the exact nature of the organic matter entering his intestine? Never mind the stuff he finally squeezes *out* of it.

But credit where credit's due. Big was into faeces long – that's literally ages – before it was really fashionable. (You're saying you don't remember all those articles in the style mags on feculence? The *I-D* defecation issue? You really *don't*? Where the hell *were* you?)

As I remember, Big must've been the world's only potty-training father who took more pride in *what* was passed (I'm talking size, shape, consistency) than in the actual *passing*. The apex of descriptive phrases in Big's bowel-related-vocabulary is (wait for it) *pellet*. The pellet – small, odourless, hard, plentiful – is the very ultimate in Big-gratification. If you use the word *pellet* in casual conversation his irises tighten. It *delights* him.

Did we rebel? Of *course* we did. We rebelled plenty. Barge especially. I mean this boy was nine years old before he knew 'cake' was a sweet thing. He was *weaned* on the rice and the oat and the fish varieties. He thought a sponge was something you washed your face with. He thought chocolate was a shade of brown. He thought nougat was . . . What *is* nougat, precisely?

And the rest of us? The *gang*? Why the hell are you asking? We're *children*. We get what we're given and like it or lump it. Sometimes both. *Everyone* knows childhood is gastronomical slavery. No surprises there.

Ironically – I know this'll kill you – that trusty Queen of Misery, M'lady Poodle, who by nature you might think would be a foodie revolutionary, is actually the most crushingly anal, hummous-spreading, sprout-eating, sugar-eschewing member of our culinary party. She is blessed with the taste-awareness of your average hard-core puritanical self-flagellator. She's a nutritional whore. She'll eat something wholemeal and then beg you for *more*.

So I'm still diligently painting Margaret's blessed mug at half-past-nine in the ping-pong chamber – a small, grim box-room which clumsily straddles the stairway between the kitchens and the foyer – while every so often an individual family member will stroll past the door clutching handfuls of macadamia nuts, tiny, parboiled cocktail sausages (100 per cent soya and *absolutely* kosher), salted anchovies and nail-thin slices of badly peeled kiwi. All in all it's a suitably high-flown and tempting gastronomical procession. But I'm not partaking. I'm *working*.

That said, I still find the time to listen in on Big informing La Roux about the ban on *Black Beauty* (so I *let slip* this little detail. It was purely accidental). He's cornered him on the stairway and he's telling him off in no uncertain terms, his voice cascading effortlessly down the sensuous curve of the walls – like the very best kind of public transport announcement – but sounding all tight-lipped and brisk and nasty.

*Poor* blighter.

In truth, I've rarely known Big take against another human being with so much mean determination. Not since Roy Jenkins turned his back on the British Labour Movement (that was in March, and it's *June* already).

The man's a messed-up liberal with strong totalitarian

tendencies, but he places a *very high premium* on natural loyalty. Which is why he loves pooches, come to think of it – loyalty's supposedly their most essential characteristic (well, loyalty and *greed*. And halitosis. And don't forget all that relentless *farting* – three things you'd have to be crazy to place any kind of premium upon).

I'm still cheerfully mulling over how badly La Roux will have taken this unexpected dose of bitter medicine when, out of the blue, at nine-forty-five precisely, he quietly enters my ping-pong kingdom (as I'm sure you can imagine, a *most* unwelcome intrusion) and does his utmost to attract my attention without actually resorting to simply *speaking*.

Still in that damned khaki boiler suit. He picks up a ping-pong bat, plays a mean air-game (he wins 21–2 – I mean, he *kills* that imaginary fucker) then lounges, slightly breathless, against the damp white wall, ditches the bat, sticks his thumbs through his belt-holes and sighs several times just a fraction too loudly. I peek up, grimace, and carry on painting.

'Big really has it in for me,' he finally grumbles, as if under some illusion that I'm in the slightest bit interested.

'How tragic,' I say, literally *dripping* with empathy.

'You could've told me about the ban on *Black Beauty*,' he mutters, 'he just completely lost it. He cornered me on the stairway – and here's the strange part – he didn't even bother pushing home a strategic advantage by standing on the stair above. Quite the opposite. He stood on the one *below*, like some kind of deeply deranged pixie, and then just completely ripped into me.

'It was frightening. I felt like I was trapped inside *Gulliver's Travels*: the part where he wakes up and a group of tiny maniacs are disabling him with string. It was really quite . . .' he pauses, 'quite *unsettling*.'

'The Lilliputians,' I shrug wisely.

'I mean, how messed-up can a four year old be?'

I glance towards him. 'Feely's just morbid. It's a phase.'

La Roux sniffs plaintively a couple of times (he's such a damn *lamb),* wanders off for a while, then returns dragging a fold-up chair behind him.

He opens it next to the table, sits down, grabs a mug and a brush, then watches my each and every move with all the unblinking concentration of a deeply transcendental iguana. I don't crack under the pressure. I don't shake, I don't whimper.

'Can I help you with this?' he says, after a rather painful few minutes. 'I think I've got the general hang of it. My hand-to-eye coordination', he swanks, 'is actually quite legendary.'

I pause and give him a steely glare.

'Help me? Why?'

He sighs. 'It's just . . .' He thinks for a while. 'It's just – how to explain it? . . . It's just *politics.* I think I need to re-establish my power base. Within the family.'

Was ever a man so rank and duplicitous?

'How?' I gasp. 'By slithering your way in *here* and ingratiating yourself with *me*?'

(Oh, come *on.* Don't be taken in by my tone. Wise *up.* Tune *in.* It's just basic girl-grandstanding.)

'Yes,' he smiles, reading me perfectly, his teeth overlapping like the yellowing slats in an old ivory-spined fan. 'Yes,' he repeats, 'you've got it *exactly*.'

Then he stares at me for a moment (okay, so I'm finally smiling. I can't *help* myself. The damn fucker's *charmed* me) and then slowly and painstakingly he starts painting some pottery.

And I'll tell you something for nothing: he's not half-bad at it, either.

So there you have it: the strangely simple story of precisely how – in case you're at *all* interested – that unashamedly high-gusseted, acne-ridden chancer known as La Roux finally wins me over with his brutal candour.

*Happy* now?

No. Of *course* I don't know what I'm getting myself into. Lighten *up* a little. Weren't you *ever* sixteen?

## 7

Interest in the hotel – all things considered – has been pretty downright bloody phenomenal. I think it's the part-island factor that really sets people a-tingle. We've had born-agains, nudists, the krishna-conscious, the military. We've had a *bona fide* Hollywood star (or just about: David Soul's masseur's mother), a school for children with learning difficulties, a famous astrologer, a football player. We've had them *all*. They've come, they've seen, they've felt the itch. But no one's really Nails-Out Scratching. Not, that is, until now.

(So I'm hardly an economist, but it suddenly feels like 1980s Britain is sweetly faltering on the quiet cusp of soon-to-be full-throttle, hard-roaring, break-the-sound-barrier booming. She's like an anxious, sherry-drenched virgin nervously considering the scary technicalities of her imminent deflowering. She's staggering. She's *teetering*.)

And sure enough (as if to vindicate my intellectual theorising), on the morning after the *impasse* before, a brand-spanking-new prospective buyer hitches a lift over to the island on the back of Black Jack's antiquated, jaw-juddering Sea Tractor (ah, how *fleeting* my fancies).

This woman has an insolent look about her. A *haughtiness*. In fact, when she dismounts it's with the ridiculously inappropriate demeanour of a small but feminized Vasco da Gama loftily laying claim to the Horn of Africa (kind of *fuck the indigens* from the outset, if you know what I mean).

As far as I can tell, Ms Penny Smolly (for that is the appellation of this paragon) is a bad-arsed but well-heeled fruit cake. More money than sense (although astonishingly mean with it), and worse still, an unadulterated *cat* lover.

Believe it or not, she actually has it in mind to transform this blameless isle into a feline sanctuary (doesn't she know cats *hate* water?) and although you wouldn't know it just to look at her – she's slight with grey eyes, an unusual strawberry-blonde moustache and a chin like a truncheon – this wench has a masters in snarling and whining.

Oh my dear *Lord*. She's already brought the poor estate agent out in an allergy (all that fur on her collar and the cuffs of her cardigan) and as she strolls about the gaff unearthing *countless* imperfections he politely punctuates her on-going invective with his quiet but chesty and *exquisitely* timed sneezing.

Big's nose (which frankly is the only really sizeable thing about him, apart from his ego, his temper and his libido) is also put out of joint royally when – on espying his current adventure in crochet: a wall-hanging of the USA with each state a different colour (that's *fifty* states in total, so naturally *someone's* gonna have to draw the short straw in relation to tincture. Texas is post-box red; Nevada, apple green; Philadelphia a sunflower yellow; Denver a bright south-sea blue; and from there on in things get a little hairy: Utah is the subtle shade of dirty bathwater; Virginia resembles a badger's scrotum; Louisiana's like a dead man's liver . . . ) – she asks him whether he ever learned to *knit* (he never did), then she promptly takes issue with his painstaking re-arrangement of the main back shrubbery.

During the following two hours she goes on to scrutinize every single intimate nook and crevice of this huge Art Deco edifice, paying more attention to fine detail than a police chief inspector (I mean, down to the extent of noting how *nine* bulbs need replacing) and is suitably appalled when in one dark corner she accidentally happens across fat Patch biting loving chunks out of Feely's dimpled, putty-coloured buttocks (purely for the hell of it. His arse is irresistible. It literally *demands* masticating).

Of course he's protesting – and powerfully – writhing like a hungry pup, absolutely *hysterical,* the plastic mug jammed firm onto his fist again, his chin already pink-tinged with carpet burn. It's like an obscene early tableau from *Caligula*.

Rather too soon after she finds me, large as life – if not *larger* – sitting cross-legged on the cocktail counter, painstakingly dissecting a troublesome verruca (I've learned over the years that if you soak your foot for long enough in slightly salted warm water and then pluck at the offending growth with tweezers, the whole organism can be extracted in one complete segment, like a perfectly-formed miniature cauliflower).

But the *real* surprise still lies quietly in wait for this punctilious Miss – like a low-slung, huge-jawed, gently growling *jaguar* – upstairs, at the very far end of the furthest top landing. *Ah, mais oui!* The lair of *La Roux*!

So they've inspected all the other suites (that's fourteen in total) and this is the last. As a precaution the agent knocks cautiously on that (by now worryingly familiar) peeling aquamarine door, hears no audible answer, enters, inhales, blanches, staggers straight to the window and flings it wide open – the smell in there is already quite extraordinary, a burning, eye-watering odour of rank antiseptic – indicates the view (it's a great one), the carpets and the original light fitments.

Catwoman snipes on about the heady aroma (she thinks something died somewhere), the hole in the ceiling, finds fault with the window-frames and bemoans the poor finish on the en-suite tiling. *Phew.* At last the inspection is finally over and they are literally *just about ready* to turn on their tails when Miss Fur-ball suddenly detects an untoward *squeaking*.

I think you know *whither*. She makes a hasty bee-line towards the stroll-in storage facility (hoping, no doubt, to add a minor infestation to her major demolition), yanks the door wide, and finds not a mouse in her house, as she'd fully anticipated, but a bad-skinned, balaclavaed, South African nest-builder spanking his pink plank in an orgy of wank, right there, large as life, just inside.

But that's not the worst of it. La Roux (the *sauce*) is employing something rather unusual as his masturbatory inspiration – his stimulus, his *trigger*. It is a photograph (old, well-worn, black and white) of a mongrel: part-chow, part-pug, part-golden labrador (when you think about it, a really horrible genetic mixture; bug-eyed, blue-tongued but with a ridiculously obliging, indeed, perhaps even *accommodating* nature).

Doesn't look good, does it? Especially to a cat lover.

La Roux can't say much as Ms Smolly gasps, curses, turns and scampers, but he does say *something* (credit him at least with the genius of brevity). In fact he says two things: the first is, 'This is not as bad as it seems. I actually *know* this animal.' The second? 'My father's a gynaecologist.'

Virtually a life history, really, when all the silly woman

actually wanted – or needed – was a rather more basic but nonetheless suitably *cringing* apology.

More fool she.

Oh *dear*. I duly deputize myself to mediate a peace between the two warring parties (that's Big and The Masturbator – Ms Penny Smolly having hissy-fitted and high-tailed it almost immediately after).

To say Big is cross hardly does proper justice to his *colossal* rage. Don't get me wrong. The man is not against masturbation *per se*. He simply thinks there's a time and a place. And This Time and This Place just don't happen to be it.

He's probably right. To try and calm him *down* I back him *up* assiduously, I chip in gamely, I parrot, I chirrup, I echo. Mrs Mary Whitehouse herself would've been hard-pressed to find a spare ounce of moral laxity in me.

Of course I have *motives ulterior*.

We happen to be conducting this particular conversation ensconced downstairs in the ladies' loo, accompanied by Feely, who is squirming on the tiling like a greased pig in a pie shop. The cold-water tap is gushing and we are struggling to hold his rapidly purpling paw beneath it. I am in charge of the mug-end, Big is in charge of his wrist, Feely is in charge of absolutely nothing, his foul temper included.

'La Roux's plainly demented,' I tell Big, turning the tap on a little harder, 'even muskrats have better instincts.'

Big stares at me suspiciously and then shakes his head. He's small but he's on the ball. He plainly smells something. My odious perfidy, probably.

'So who *cares*', I continue, 'if his stupid father delivered

Feely? What does it matter? That was four whole years ago. And look what a nightmarish liability *he* turned into.'

I give the mug a twist and a yank. Feely yowls. It loosens a fraction. I push it under the tap again. My stomach is soaking.

Big adjusts his position. 'Why not give me a break', he growls, 'from your pathetic attempts at reverse psychology? You seem to forget that I'm the same old man who spends his time watching that ginger moron Denis Waterman displaying five times your level of clumsy fudge in *The* bloody *Sweeney*.'

My head snaps back. 'Waterman's a blonde,' I gurgle.

'From where I'm standing', Big continues, 'it's very clear that this devious South African has somehow managed – no *conspired* – to win you over. Heaven alone knows how or why, but he's done it.'

Well I *never*. I'm so astonished by Big's unexpected gust of insight that my grip momentarily relaxes. He notices. 'Don't let up,' he grumbles, 'keep trying. I think it's finally coming.'

I still don't react. He peers up at me, morosely.

'Uh . . . that's probably exactly what Penny Smolly was thinking,' I splutter.

Big does not smile. He's struggling to keep Feely's wrist firm. Feely has helpfully removed all the weight from his feet and is now just poignantly dangling. I get into gear and twist again. As I do so I feel a very gradual easing. Then *pop*! It's out.

Not his hand, unfortunately, but his shoulder bone, which slips from its socket with all the smooth ease of a bloated bee from a bluebell. Except not nearly so quietly. In fact the astonishing howl this four year old promptly delivers would strike envy into the hearts of a hundred-strong convention of Primal Screamers. He literally *bellows*.

*Yikes!* We both drop him so fast it's like he's suddenly on fire, and the poor kid's barely hit the floor (with a bang) before he's up on his feet again and hopping around the *ladies* like a badly-injured baby ape, his entire right arm and shoulder hanging completely off-kilter. It's *hideous*.

Big (always an ass in a crisis) flies into an immediate panic. The tide's in. The tractor's out. How the heck will we manage to get the doctor over? I'm still pathetically fumbling to turn that damn tap off like a sweaty-pawed, slack-jawed, cack-handed water lover (like father, like daughter). All is chaos.

Then suddenly something rather magnificent happens. As if from nowhere (okay, it seems likely the little pervert was hiding in a cubicle all the while, but I only actually realize this after), La Roux crashes into our crazy-palpitating, terror-struck environs, catches a firm hold of Feely, slams him down onto the floor, straightens his back, grabs his shoulder, gets him to count to three, applies a monumentally well-judged amount of force (but only very briefly) to the offending region, and then *click*, manages to shunt that pesky bone straight back into its socket again.

The whole affair takes approximately seven seconds. In fact the drama's all over so quickly that Feely can't help feeling a fraction disgruntled and yanks the plastic mug off his fist just to facilitate his socking La Roux a firm blow with it.

La Roux takes his thrashing like a man (upon his knee – he's standing already), folds his arms anxiously across his puny chest (in the intimidating face of Big's astonished gaze) and says – his tone almost apologetic – 'I trained as a medic in the South African Army.'

*Army?*

'Somebody, somewhere trusted this misfit with a *firearm*?'

(So I thought I was just *thinking*, but in the heat of the moment I find my mouth is moving and I am actually *speaking*.)

La Roux sticks out his chin. 'I said I was a *medic*,' he repeats. 'My most essential weapons – aside from my trusty pill box and my hypodermic syringe – were my natural cunning, my fierce intelligence . . .' he pauses, '. . . and my cast-iron stomach, obviously.'

Feely takes this rather appropriate opportunity to deal him a further well-aimed blow, then drops the mug, sits down squarely on the cold tiles and commences a brand-new (and very lengthy) phase of uninhibited howling.

Big, clucking like a mother hen, bends over to pick him up. I turn briefly to try and wring out my soaking skirt (wool's so appallingly absorbent, don't you find?), and when I finally chance to glance his way again, our diabolical hero – sweet and silent as a dark Red Admiral on a soft sea breeze – has bashfully flitted.

Hell's bells. Events are certainly progressing at a fair old whack: especially *strategically*. I mean, one minute things are looking rather bleak for that cheerfully conniving South African buffoon, and then, in the very next instant, his fortunes have altered course completely.

It's like a critical scene in a TV drama where the character you couldn't help liking the best suddenly turns out to be the self-same bastard who viciously murdered his best friend's budgerigar. Only back to front (which would have to make him the person you like *least* offering a timely portion of mouth-to-beak resuscitation).

Oh, liven *up*, you *know* what I mean.

Initially it's rather difficult to gauge the subtle shifts and slides in La Roux's general household popularity. Patch – having been anything from lacklustre to indifferent previous to the Feely disaster – now thinks the sun shines out of this medically trained impostor's most intimate orifice.

Big has been briefly – if not entirely convincingly – won over. Feely – now here's the weird part – having liked La Roux from the outset, suddenly can't bear to catch the slightest *whiff* of him. And me? I liked the fool before, and now I love him ever more dearly.

These feelings are – if anything – intensified by a small and ridiculous incident which occurs later that self-same evening. Having espied La Roux's miniature guitar in his nest the day before, I suggest (with the secret aim of mollifying Feely a little) that we all get together that night, once my lengthy stint of painting is over, for a spot of musical revelry.

The whole family just *loves* to warble. Unfortunately we possess not a single harmonious bone between us. We have voices like chainsaws. In gloriously cacophonous union we're sufficiently discordant to unhinge a raven (except, that is, for Barge, who sang like a nightingale prior to becoming tragically tonedeaf aged nine after firing off a cap gun inside his ear to forestall a riotous stint in some degraded, robe-wearing atoll-based version of the Vienna Boy's Choir. The clever nipper).

At half past eight we all assemble in the Palm Court – a glorified greenhouse which adjoins my sleeping quarters. Big thinks the large glass surround will make the acoustics spectacular. La Roux duly arrives (a little later than the rest of us, swathed in a dusty red velvet curtain garnered from one of the upstairs toilets, resembling a half-cocked thrift-shop Roman emperor), his small guitar ensconced snugly under his plush-draped arm.

As chief musician, he immediately takes possession of the best (if also the most arse-clenchingly uncomfortable – the man's all *show*) high-backed bamboo chair available. The rest of us cluster around him, balanced precariously on ill-maintained, mouldy-cushioned garden furniture.

Feely naturally has his bean-bag with him, but refuses to sit upon it. Instead he crouches suspiciously on the parquet and clutches it to his chest as if living in a constant state of dread that La Roux will suddenly and arbitrarily snatch it from him, hurl it to the floor and conduct some agonizing experiment upon it.

La Roux makes a meal out of tuning up his instrument (a skinny bare knee and a tantalizing flash of thigh just visible from beneath his crude acres of velvet) while the rest of us debate which songs we'll be singing.

Big – for reasons which will probably always remain a mystery to any person of taste or intelligence – is rather keen to wrap his tonsils around Cliff Richard's 'Living Doll', Patch has set her heart on Kate Bush's 'Babooshka', Feely demands Chas and Dave's 'Rabbit'. I suggest 'The Art of Parties' by Japan just to show how highbrow I am. But no one – least of all the guitar-player – seems to appreciate how clever I'm being.

In the end a compromise is reached when Patch suggests this year's Eurovision smash: Bucks Fizz's 'Making Your Mind Up' (sweet Jesus, how *unifying*), and even though I hold out against it with ugly oodles of teen-determination, the majority still somehow maintains its sway (Yeah, so *fuck* Euro-democracy).

68

La Roux, on being asked whether he'd be all right to strum this tune, modestly acknowledges that he can play 'by ear only'. We are all suitably impressed – to the extent that Big asks him, just once, to adjust his curtains after they gape even further to reveal a slightly off-putting pair of capacious white y-fronts, and even then in a voice you might almost call *indulgent*.

We illustrate our sing-a-long expertise by clapping out an approximate beat to start off with (two minutes are wasted deciding the appropriate tempo) then I duly deputize myself to count us all in. *One, two, three, FOUR*. And we're off.

Patch is immediately on her feet doing the requisite Euro-band hand movements. Feely – still clutching his bean-bag like it's his dancing partner – is performing a marvellously seductive baby wiggle. Big is all smiles. It's a *party*.

But it doesn't last. Barely a single verse is completed before everything descends inexorably into chaos. La Roux is banging out an unbearably noxious racket on his guitar (which while small in stature is still large on volume). He would appear to possess no musical talent *whatsoever*.

Big is the first to really discern it (the man actively *relishes* disappointment). 'I thought', he says stiffly, 'you said you could play that thing.'

La Roux stops his horrible strumming. He thinks hard for a while, then he shakes his head, slowly. 'Uh . . .' he pauses, as if deeply confused by our plain irritation. 'Uh, no,' he smiles, 'I don't think I ever said I could *play*.'

'Not *anything*?' Patch asks.

'So why', Big interrupts, 'do you own a guitar?'

La Roux looks down at the offending object? 'This old thing?'

We all nod in unison. He shrugs. 'I stole it off a child on the train.' He frowns. 'A very *bad* child.'

Big abruptly clambers to his feet and marches outside onto the wide sweep of the hotel's grand balcony. Patch scratches her head. 'Wow,' she mumbles (and it's almost in *awe*), 'what a complete and utter *embarrassment* you are.'

Feely is staring at the guitar with worried eyes as he stands behind a bamboo, glass-topped table, making a meal out of the contents of his nasal passages. He plainly has La Roux down as a certifiable child-hater.

La Roux adjusts his robe. 'You know something?' he whispers confidentially. 'I find your family unusually uptight for a bunch of hippies.'

I say nothing (What's *to* say?).

'And the worst part is,' he continues, 'I could've learned the guitar as a boy, but I missed my opportunity. I actually went and took swimming lessons instead.'

'Really?' I ask gamely. 'And are you an impressive swimmer?'

He blinks. 'Swimmer? *Me?!*' He chuckles. 'No. I could never get my head around the basic knack of . . .' he thinks for a while, '. . . the knack of *floating*.'

For a few, brief seconds he silently mulls over this poignant irony, then he smiles, stands up, passes me the guitar, yawns, gathers his red robe grandly around him and glides off with all the mile-high airs and inappropriate graces of an unkempt, over-indulged *Folies Bergère*.

Would you believe it? The cheeky *freak*.

70

# 8

It's mid-morning, low-tide, and I'm taking La Roux on a tour of this tiny island's most tantalizing rock pools. La Roux has recently divulged an unusual interest in crustaceans.

'I find that the happy sight of a little crab or a shrimp or a lobster', he pontificates cheerily, 'will always set me up nicely.'

Set him up for *what* exactly, he doesn't deign to specify.

And he still persists in wearing his balaclava, even though the air is intoxicatingly soft and camomile-scented and balmy. That said, his sharp eyes peer out from behind their black woollen prison as bright and keen as a Siamese fighting rat's, and his two feet on the slippy rocks have such a confidently sure-hoofed and nimble character that to all intents and purposes they seem virtually cloven. In general, his demeanour is one of infuriatingly uninhibited perkiness.

He is strangely attired in a thin, well-worn, pale-blue summer sweater with a ill-preserved embroidered illustration of an Appaloosan pony on the front of it, and some light, canvas-coloured baggy trousers, so low on the hips and wide on the thigh that it's as if he has a small section of a trellis stuck up inside of them. They may well be African in origin, or perhaps even Indian.

Naturally his unorthodox garb means he receives a couple of slightly perturbed sideways glances from the occasional sharp-eyed but nonetheless deeply inconsequential tourist –

and if they're staring at *me*, coincidentally, then they're simply marvelling at my loose, well-worn, brown leather pedal-pushers matched with a scant but utterly modest cheesecloth halter – *either* way, he doesn't seem to notice.

Slightly *more* perturbing, though, is the shadowy figure of Black Jack leaning heavily on the fence near the Pilchard Inn, glaring pointedly down in our general direction.

La Roux gives a fine impression of complete self-absorption as he shuffles carefully around the edge of a good-sized pool, squats and peers (He has painstakingly fashioned a pokey stick from a stray twig and has already become ludicrously attached to this implement which he swishes and waves whenever the opportunity presents itself).

'See anything?'

He doesn't answer. He lifts some yellowing flotsam with his twig, shifts slightly, and stares some more. While he's quietly preoccupied I resolve to ask him some leading questions.

'I imagine you must've lived quite close to the sea in Cape Town. The city's right on the coast, isn't it?' I begin with.

'Must I?' he answers haughtily. '*Is* it?'

He clearly doesn't appreciate this particular line of questioning.

'And your father's a gynaecologist.'

La Roux unbuckles his sandles, pulls off his socks, then laboriously rolls up his canvas trousers. His legs are phenomenally ginger-hairy against a contrasting skin-tone on the bright-white side of feta.

His two feet are practically skeletal and in the dry morning heat the aroma from his absurdly long toes hinges on the fragile cusp of sweet Swiss-cheesy. He tests the pool's temperature with the tip of his fingers, then clambers in.

The water hits just under his knee. He shuffles around awhile, sending everything cloudy, then he pauses.

'I remember Christmas mornings,' he whispers suddenly. 'My father, as always, up early and working at the large oak bureau in the sitting-room, waiting for me and my brother, the tree lights twinkling, the presents wrapped, paging and paging through a thousand graphic gynaecological illustrations of chronically diseased wombs and vaginas.'

My face creases.

'I'm starting to wonder,' he continues, glancing over his shoulder for a second, 'whether Black Jack might be sexually *inverted*.'

I continue frowning. 'Inverted? What does that mean?'

'A lover of men.'

'*Jack?* Never.'

'It's just that he *will* keep staring.'

I frown (I mean how to put this *politely*?). 'Perhaps it's your balaclava. It does give you a slightly intimidating aura.'

'No.' La Roux shakes his scraggy head firmly. 'It goes deeper. It's something . . .' he thinks for a moment, '. . .something untapped, something underneath, something . . . something *goosy*.'

*Goosy?*

'Jack? *Untapped?*' I cackle. 'That's *twisted*.'

La Roux swaps his stick into his other hand and then proceeds to wave it in Jack's general direction. Jack freezes and turns briefly to peer behind him. Luckily Patch and Feely are just within sight carrying the nets to the tennis court.

'It has subsequently become very difficult for me', La Roux

continues, 'to even *think* about a woman's sexual and reproductive organs without experiencing strong feelings of fear and revulsion. And believe it or not, in certain *especially* intimate situations, I find I lose all sensation in the pads of my fingers.'

I frown. 'That's just *tragic*.'

La Roux nods, sadly, plainly immune to my withering sarcasm. 'When I asked him about it, the family doctor said the only way to get over this problem was to reacquaint myself with the vagina, but in what he called a gentle, open and *unthreatening* environment. By a process of calmly inspecting and slowly re-educating. Just *glimpsing* . . .'

He gives me a sudden, furtive glance, to see how he's doing (Who does he think he's *kidding*?). My face is a surly mask of violent antipathy. I think he gets the message.

'Anyway,' he chuckles wryly, 'in many respects I see this strange affliction as the ultimate festive offering from my father.'

'Give me a *Chopper* any day,' I mutter.

He points his stick accusingly. 'You're still such a *baby*.'

I scowl back.

'In defence of the vagina,' I tell him, watching indulgently as he bends over and tries but fails to dismantle a limpet, 'I'm pretty certain men's genitals do their own fair share of rotting and festering.'

La Roux's eyes widen. 'Are you trying to destroy my sexual impulses *altogether*?' he whispers hoarsely. I can't tell if he's joking. He straightens up, wipes his fingers on his trousers and shuffles around some more with a curiously unconvincing tragic air about him.

After a brief lull he pauses. 'When I was a kid,' he begins

74

dreamily, 'I once went on holiday to a farm in the Orange Free State . . .'

'A place full of liberated citrus, presumably,' I wisecrack. He yanks up his balaclava so that I can now observe his thin lips moving.

'That was *pathetic*,' his disembodied mouth informs me, then he carefully readjusts his head-gear to its former position. 'Anyhow,' he continues, 'they had a water hole – we called it a *Boer* hole – it was like a pond, only above the ground and large – five or six metres in diameter – and round but not too deep. Concrete. Like a murky swimming-pool. Full of all kinds of crap. And I'd climb into it on hot days and romp about.

'One day I clambered in and I was lounging against the edge, just relaxing, when suddenly a huge fish swam between my legs . . .' He catches my expression. 'I mean, my calves and my knees. And it got trapped there. Only briefly.'

'I've had porcupines graze my shins before,' I immediately trump him, 'and I was stung by a jellyfish once on my thigh, and my leg blew up like it was badly scalded. Not here, obviously, but in an obscure region of northern Madagascar.'

La Roux is patently not the slightest bit interested. 'In truth I think it was the single most *happy* moment of my life,' he continues, his voice still seductively blissful, 'to feel the weed in the water, the hot sun on my skin and that frantic fish just . . . just wriggling.'

He pauses. 'Oh dear me,' he mutters conspiratorially, his voice immediately dropping by half an octave. 'Black Jack's approaching.'

'It doesn't happen often,' I tell him, finally getting into the swing of things, 'but sometimes when you're floating in the

Mermaid Cove, over on the other side of the island, you occasionally get to feel the fish in the water.'

His eyes widen. 'On your lower limbs *specifically*?'

'Yes. Sometimes they burrow into the sandy shingle and you find yourself treading on them. And sometimes they glance off your arms when you're swimming. But usually only tiddlers.'

'I don't swim,' he reminds me.

'Or even if you're just paddling.'

He scowls. 'I don't *paddle*.'

I struggle obligingly to recall the word he'd used previously. 'When you *romp* then,' I exclaim, 'when you're *romping*.'

Jack is now standing just a few feet away from us. He's still on the firm sand at the edge of the rocky section. He doesn't want to trouble himself with clambering over. La Roux sniffs, turns away and continues wading. I nod half-heartedly.

'I think you'd better tell your father,' Jack shouts, clearly not at all affected by his apathetic reception, 'that a segment of the cliff-top fencing next to the old chapel has just gone missing. He'll need to replace it before some idiot tourist topples over.'

While Jack is speaking La Roux tickles me distractingly behind my knee with the fiendishly scratchy tip of his damp twig. 'Ask him,' he suddenly whispers, when I turn defensively and slap the spot, 'whether Jack is short for anything.'

'Sorry?' (Inside me an angry dialogue is being conducted between my breasts and my brain – that *bastard* stick has only gone and made my nipples tighten!)

'Go *on*,' he hisses, 'just *ask* him.'

I clear my throat and cross my arms (These are pre-Lycra days, *smart-arse*, and I'm wearing a semi-translucent pale halter top. It's turning into an intimate Armageddon down there – my aureoles darkening dramatically, my nipples jutting like tent-pegs . . . ). 'La Roux here was just wondering,' I say loudly (perhaps, under the circumstances, without sufficient due-consideration), 'whether the name Jack is actually short for anything.'

La Roux, once again, has his back to me, but I think I can detect his bony shoulders shaking. Jack scowls. 'What do you mean?'

I turn to La Roux again. 'He wants to know what you mean exactly.'

La Roux's shoulders are now shuddering uncontrollably.

'What does he mean, *short for anything*?' Jack repeats.

I shrug limply.

A minute's uneasy silence commences, only punctuated by La Roux's hysterical snuffling. When the minute is over, and the tension's just about to diffuse, La Roux contains his inexplicable excitement for just long enough to heighten it again. 'I was only idly wondering,' he creaks, 'whether it was *short* for anything.'

Jack is quiet for a moment. He looks down at his feet, as if he is actually, *physically* walking the fine line between fury and bemusement.

'Whether *what* is short for anything?' he answers finally.

La Roux starts laughing again. 'Your *name*,' he splutters.

Jack takes a small step forward. His fists are slowly clenching and unclenching. His brown cheeks are suddenly livid.

'I just *wondered*,' La Roux bellows, throwing out his arms and twirling his stick infuriatingly, 'I just *wondered* about your name.'

Jack carefully lifts his right foot up on to the rocks, then pauses, his large bulk swaying. He's like a huge, newly blinded bison slowly negotiating the scarily multifarious world around him. Trying. Failing.

For the first time – as he sniffs and blinks in a curiously affecting slow motion – I see that he's actually *fragile*. A mesmerizing mix of the distressingly magisterial and the irredeemably bovine (well, *hell*, it worked for John Wayne all those years).

After a few loose moments he gradually gathers himself together. 'I'm going fishing tomorrow morning, Medve,' he announces, turning to me directly and in the process cutting that rude dog La Roux completely.

*Medve.* My bare toes curl into the rock and muck and weed. It's gentle weather but I'm very nearly blown away. *Black Jack just used my name for the first time ever!* And so naturally, too, like he's been secretly rehearsing it in private or something.

La Roux responds by emitting a series of musical burps. He can apparently do this to order.

'About five,' Jack continues stiffly, 'in the little boat, if you fancy it.'

I nod again. 'Well, I'll certainly think it over. Thanks.'

He removes his foot, smiles thinly, turns and leaves.

Well I *never*.

La Roux, meanwhile, has sat himself down on the edge of the pool with his two feet dangling into the shallow water. 'Medve! *Medve*, quickly!' he whispers. '*Quickly.* Come here.'

He has his hands tightly cupped on his lap as if he's captured a small but skittish crustacean. His balaclava has been pulled up, off his face, and is now balanced on top of his head

– still maintaining its shape – like some weirdly cylindrical mobile chimney.

'Jesus!' he exclaims delightedly. 'It's really *tickling*! Come *on*. Come quickly, before it gets away.'

I stagger across the slippy rocks and join him. I squat down and peer.

'Show.'

'I'm not sure what it *is* exactly,' he whispers, his keen thin lips dripping in anticipation.

'Probably a common shrimp,' I debunk. 'I thought I caught a glimpse of one earlier.'

'It's entirely possible. *Look*.'

He opens his cupped hands gradually. I stare hard. Then harder still. His pale fingers are gently surrounding a little red organism, a mollusc, a soft thing. A deep sea creature . . .

I blink. A brief flash follows. The shutter lifts.

What that cheeky varmint is *actually* cradling is the disembodied, yanked back, grinning tip of his unrepentantly uncut, small-eyed, purple-lipped pecker.

La Roux blinks up at me, his wool-blotched face suffused in a childlike glow of absolute – almost *bewildered* – wonderment (He's like a favourite nephew offering his ancient aunt his very last piece of toffee brittle. It's *appalling*).

I grit my teeth. I steady my feet. I clear my throat. I *balance* internally. Then: 'My *God*,' I whisper gently, my face a profoundly sympathetic mask of quite the *tenderest* bewilderment. 'La Roux, my *God*! It's so very *ugly*. And tiny too, *really* tiny.'

His smile falters. And while it's faltering, with a single hefty kick from my huge left hoof I shove that ginger-haired and deeply perverted mother-fucker straight down, head first, into the water.

You know what? In my trivial pursuit of the fine 1980s Free Enterprise Ethic, I'm seriously considering establishing my very own International Library of Gullibility – kind of along the same lines as The School of Hard Knocks, but warmer, and friendlier and with unlimited lending.

Think there's any future in it? Better still, fancy *joining*?

## 9

Don't ask me why, but I suddenly feel like the time is prime to get something rather *hefty* off my 38B (that's my chest measurement, you *booby*), both on behalf of my huge-hoofed self and my dilapidated family.

Unorthodox we may well be. Laughing-stocks? Certainly. Eccentric? Eclectic? Erratic? Entopic? (We can do all the 'e's without even *blinking*.)

*Yeah*, so we're the first to chuckle at our own endless inadequacies, but when everything's finally said and done, we still take great umbrage at the insulting suggestion that we're completely *obsessed* by crass anality (I mean, did I even yet make *mention* of my capacious anus?).*

It just so happens that there are some things, some . . . how to put it? . . . some *cracks* in the plaster, some *issues* (Big's gut, his pedantry, my mail-order addiction, Poodle's tiny breasts, Barge's beet-boiling) which just won't budge or shift no matter how hard or how diligently you try to paper them over. And that *anus probus*, I fear, is clearly no exception.

Right. So *I know* it's a subject which we have all – so far and so *assiduously* – been avoiding, but when it actually comes down to it the only real problem with Mo's mighty invention is that there *is* no real problem (and I have a powerful teenage yen for exaggeration).

The Anal Probe – *Sick*, you're thinking? *Weird? Shameful?*

*Saucy? Problematic? Traumatic?* Nah! I know it sounds crazy, but the inescapably tedious truth of the matter is that the Probe is nothing more creepy or glorious than an actual-factual, down-to-earth, dull-as-dishwater metal detector: a plain plastic chair (and there's nothing remotely *invasive*) which, when you sit down upon it, kindly informs a disinterested observer whether there's anything *remiss* clenched inside your cavities (and I don't exactly mean your *teeth* here, either).

Mo says the results are nothing short of fantastic. During a trial run in Idaho's main female prison one woman was apprehended with six razor blades lodged inside her vagina, all neatly wrapped in a small, neat sheath of protective plastic (some indication – if any were needed – of the sheer lengths these girls will go to to avoid unsightly stubble).

Not only an absolute boon for the prison authorities, a smart innovation and a serious time-saver, the Probe also – in *real* terms – means a serious reduction in rubber-glove expenditure (*Lord!* To hear me flog this pony you'd think I was on commission). And last, but certainly not least, it's a *huge* potential money-spinner for my dear mother Mo and her shifty, lily-livered, liberally inclined, financial and ideological partner, Bob Ranger.

(I'd rather not dwell, if you don't mind, on the tough early days of this fine device's preparatory testing regimen. Just whisper the dread words *metal pessary* within earshot and my eyes begin watering – although, on the upside, my powerful vaginal muscles could choke a weasel.)

And that, as they say, is basically the sum of it. So how's about we all try and set our sordid minds to finally putting this whole damn Probe thing *behind* us?

82

Ah-hah-*hem*. If you get my meaning.

Talk about a whole host of *weird shit*. I've hardly set a well-turned toe back inside the hotel foyer again before Little Big Man lunges out unexpectedly from behind a ludicrously monumental translucent pink glass statue of Diana the Huntress (a goddess with huskies. For some reason they seemed to *dote* on this crazy broad way back in the thirties. I'm uncertain of her eighties status, but whenever we're engulfed by a spot of DIY chaos, Diana's always the first thing to split the scene on a series of specially-adapted squeaky cas-tors. The girl's an ancient, godly, dog-infested, iced-glass *absconder*).

He grabs a tight hold of me and spirits me off into a quiet corner. He has a deranged air, Polyfilla-coated fingers and is clutching a telegram from our dear mother Mo. He hands it over (there's hardly any sticky residue) and kindly but firmly obliges me to read it.

Here's what it says:

*Oh my sweet darling I need more money. Please, please strong-arm the lovely S. African. To hell with principle! Am on the cusp of reforming greatness! Clever Bob R. has made serious contacts with a major international security manufacturer. Wahhh! Still prison visiting. Tell kids J. H. got parole last week June 5. God Bless Norman Mailer! All is madness. Mo*

'J. H.? Who's that, then?' I ask stupidly, once I've carefully completed my scrupulous re-reading.

Big scowls. 'Abbott. The mass murderer. The *writer*.'

I make the connection. 'Ah, you mean . . .'

83

'Yes. And that's another thing,' Big rapidly continues (having failed to tell me the first thing first), 'I don't need Patch filling her silly head with a pointless heap of anti-establishment propaganda. I need you to get that book off her.'

'And then what?' I chortle. *'Burn* it?'

He's so pent-up, he can't even tell I'm joking. He just nods his agreement and then suddenly stiffens. 'Just do something for once,' he yells, 'without *bloody arguing.'*

I stare down at him for a moment. He seems barely recognizable.

'I'm sorry,' I say plaintively, 'but I can't help feeling like I'm not *getting* something.'

(I mean, either the man's displacing for some reason or his fuse has sparked out and short-circuited his sanity.) He frowns for a minute, then shrugs, then shakes his head. 'I miss Barge,' he mutters weakly, touching his hands to his temples and inadvertently war-painting them. 'And I miss Poodle. It's nothing against you, nothing *personal,* they're just that tiny little bit older and, well, *wiser.'*

He indicates a short inch between his thumb and his index finger (This is *Barge* we're talking about: a twenty-three-year-old man wholly incapable of expressing himself artistically in anything even *loosely* amounting to 3D, an atheist *pumpkin,* a salivating *ninny*).

Yeah. Thanks a bunch. So I'm sixteen years young, criminally undervalued and *hurting,* but I still take the requisite time out to carefully re-inspect that unenlightening telegram.

'I don't quite understand the South African thing. Strong arm *who* for money? Does she mean La Roux? Is he loaded or something?'

Big takes a deep breath. 'Not La Roux. She means his father.'

'Uh . . .' I frown. 'Sorry. I'm still not following.'

He snatches the telegram and carefully refolds it. 'La Roux's staying here illegally,' he whispers, all *sotto*. 'He's meant to be fighting in a war with Angola. He's AWOL. He's done a runner.'

'La Roux fighting a *war*?' I bellow, and then instantly start sniggering. '*La Roux?* Perhaps it's just me, but I find it rather difficult to picture a big . . .' (I pause, and scrabble) '. . . a big *goose* like him engaged in violent hand to hand conflict with *anybody*, let alone the marshalled armed forces of an entire British colony.'

(In my mind I have a sudden vision of La Roux in his strangely structured trousers and Appaloosan pony sweater thumbing his nose idly at ten thousand well-armed Angolan warriors. It's a huge *joke*. It must be.)

Big waves his hand. 'It's an ex-*German* colony, if you must know, and more in the style of a guerilla conflict,' he says airily, as if this explains everything.

'Wow,' I muse. 'Real guerillas? How wonderfully *African*.'

Big spends a difficult thirty seconds struggling to comprehend my position. And then, when he thinks he's finally got it (I'm just a scab he's idly peeling), the tight set of his expression implies that it's a standpoint hardly *worth* comprehending.

'Perhaps you might bear in mind', he snipes meanly, 'that there's nothing remotely *wonderful* about evading your duties, bludging off complete strangers, masturbating at will and strong-arming miniature guitars from defenceless children.'

'*Bludging?*' I blink anxiously at Big's ferocity. 'I thought you just said his dad was paying.'

'And another thing,' Big adds, ignoring my sneaky intervention, 'and it's something you might do well to try and
remember . . .' (I hold my breath and listen, appalled, as
always, to be in the direct firing line of a parental pronounce-
ment.) 'There's nothing more *sickening*', he growls emphati-
cally, 'than the spectre of science *parading* as morality.'

He pauses dramatically. 'Remember the nuclear bomb?'

I nod.

'Remember the electric chair?'

I kick the wall, gently.

'When you start combining ethics and science, no matter
how clever you are or how worthy your intentions, you
invariably end up sharing an agenda with the likes of Doctor
Mengele.'

I widen my eyes, coquettishly. 'And is that a *good* thing?'

He stares at me, briefly, then puts his hand to his stomach,
winces, and heads, at speed, towards the downstairs toilet.

Uh-*oh*. The ulcer.

As soon as Big's off barfing, I start sniffing around for my
little sister. Because *you* know and *I* know that every demon
twelve year old that ever yet filled their mean lungs with free
oxygen on God's Great Earth has a set of ears on them like a
radar-rigged, sound-sensitive hyena.

And that scurrilous Patch is truly no exception (put it this
way: if ever you're having a private conversation – if *confi-
dences* are quietly being exchanged – then that fat brat will
almost certainly be skulking somewhere within earshot).

In this instance I don't even have to look any real distance to
unearth her. She's secreted snugly inside the hotel lift (100 per
cent out of service) earwigging like a hyperactive Sugar Glider

(a nocturnal Antipodean tree rat. Have you *never* thought of investing in the *National Geographic*?).

Feely is crammed in there with her, pressing at the buttons (for all the damn good it's doing him). I yank the door open and peer in at them through the metal shutter.

'So I need an opinion on this weird telegram,' I tell her. 'Fancy providing one?'

She frowns, unhelpfully. 'I've got a pot of dhal boiling dry on the cooker. Might you consider making do, for the time being, with a list of recommended reading matter?' (The girl's such a *swot*.)

'Hmmmn. What volumes do you have in mind, specifically?'

She thinks for a moment. 'Uh . . . a social and political history of apartheid South Africa, for starters. Something short by Desmond Wilcox on human behaviour. *The Female Eunuch* – Germaine Greer.'

'Any Thurber?'

She shakes her head.

'Marilyn French, *The Women's Room*?'

The twelve year old sneers. 'So fucking *seventies*!'

'And *Jack Henry Abbott*?' I enunciate clearly.

She scowls. 'To call him a mass murderer! I mean the sheer *prejudice* of the man! He simply killed one con and seriously injured another in an act of absolutely *righteous* self-defence. Then the bastards slapped him with a *maximum sentence . . .*'

'Before you go on and break my heart completely,' I intervene, 'Mo says he got early probation last Friday.'

This emphatic sprout looks briefly delighted, then she frowns. 'So,' she sighs tiredly, 'Big still thinks Mo's screwing Bob Ranger, then?'

I nod. 'The man's such a pathetic *Sultan*. Did you hear his crazy "don't mix science and morality" speech?'

She sniggers. 'Good job you didn't bring up the invention of penicillin. That would've really *fucked* with his logic.'

'In truth,' I lie, 'I seriously thought about it.'

She pulls herself together and glances regretfully down at little Feely. 'Well, I guess I'd better start thinking about getting back to the kitchens.'

I step sideways. 'Make sure lunch is something digestible. Big-Man-No-Stomach is definitely on the warpath.'

She pulls open the metal gate. 'I'll tell you something for nothing . . .' she says, sliding quickly on past me.

I raise my brow. 'So pray *tell*.'

As she trundles towards the downstairs kitchens, yanking Feely like a small teddy behind her, she tosses some crucial information over her pudgy shoulder. 'Angola, you fucking *moron*, is a *Portuguese* colony.'

On the stairs I hear her smartly asking, 'I mean, what is *up* with that girl's history?'

But from where I'm standing, diplomatic little Feely isn't heard to answer.

* My *capacious anus*?! Wise *up*, you blimp.

## 10

La Roux has this absolutely *infuriating* way of eating. How to describe it? Instead of using his molars for chewing and grinding – like the Good Lord intended – he much prefers to employ his incisors (the sharp, foreteeth, principally designed to bite and to cut) for the main body of his masticatory work.

It's a very messy business: try and imagine a scenario where his thin lips and his sharp tongue are constantly at battle for the ultimate custody of his overall eating process (with his chin and his shirt-front this squalid dispute's main casualty), or simply visualize an eerie but rather noisy mixture of sucking and muttering (an irritable fruit bat harshly reprimanding an encroaching tree snake whilst simultaneously laying waste to an overripe fig). Either way, it's pretty *gruesome*.

Obviously, as far as Feely's concerned, La Roux's complex and unusual ingestive routine is *completely* mesmerizing. And even Patch's extremely cynical, grub-loving eyes can sometimes be seen to leave the precious confines of her own high-piled plate and to flitter, inquisitively, towards La Roux's voluble but hard-working mandibles.

On my many world-wide travels, I was once privileged to witness some freshwater piranha frenziedly devouring a baby stork who'd fallen from his nest on high – most tragically – and down into the cruelly infested water below. From brand-new flesh, keen squawk, bright eye and fine feather to bare, pale beak and chalky bone, the whole stripping and dismantling process took less than twelve brief seconds.

Unfortunately for us, La Roux is not blessed with quite this high level of digestive efficiency. He tends to take just *a little* longer.

So it's lunch-time, and we're all perched – shoved up close, like house-martins on a phone line – thigh against thigh upon two small benches (La Roux and I on one side, Feely and Patch on the other: Big is yet to join us), our elbows clashing like unwieldy, flesh-tipped fencing swords as we struggle for territory around the tiny, thick-slatted, fold-up table which has been temporarily situated by pesky Patch in the creaking bow of that big-beamed, portholed Ganges Room for the short duration of our lunching.

We are consuming a veritable feast of cold bottled, well-preserved winter vegetables: whole beet, dark spinach, red onions, fibrous celery, sweet potatoes. Served with warm dhal made from leeks and red lentils. Natural yoghurt. Unleavened bread – some strange, ill-formed, oily *paratha*, badly wound into snail-shell-curls by the clumsy hands of little Feely.

Big joins us once we've already begun to apportion, squabble and guzzle, carrying a tray of five clay mugs and a jug of water cut with salt and fresh lemon. He places it on the table and squeezes in next to Feely. Feely shunts along resentfully, whining like a disgruntled chihuahua.

From the corner of my eye (full-blown visual contact has, as yet, been carefully avoided: to meet an angry animal's gaze is *always* dangerous and I'm still keenly fearing a random strike of sudden retribution), La Roux's hair seems unusually feathered-up and wispy (I guess the sun must've dried it), but the rest of him hasn't remained quite so unaffected by his earlier misadventure.

My rapid glances detect traces of damp around his armpits and (*a-hem*) his fly. He has his favourite twig with him, however, caught and held between his bony knees.

'So what happened to your back?' Big asks, casually, picking up a spoon and dipping it into his dhal. We all look up. La Roux blinks. '*My* back?' he asks, as if certain Big must be making conversation with another, far more significant individual.

'Well, nobody else at this table, so far as I've noticed,' Big observes drily, 'has an extra-large, weed-green footprint on their sweater.'

He leans out on the bench and stares – just for effect – at the un-printed backs of Patch and Feely.

'Nope. No bigfoots there.'

La Roux twists his head to try and peer over his own shoulder. Then he stops trying and takes a large and evasive mouthful of beetroot. 'I can only imagine', he speaks with crimson-lipped muffledness, 'that I must've been kicked unexpectedly.'

'And why, I wonder, might anyone have felt the urge to do *that*?' Big asks (the tone of his voice strongly implying that there could be few activities in the whole world he himself might relish more).

La Roux shrugs and then shoots a mean sideways glance at me. 'I'm afraid I have no plain answers, sir.'

Patch nudges Feely, who is staring across the table at La Roux, his small mouth held open in a swoop of drooping wonderment. Big grunts and commences eating. His mood is patently still wholesale *stinky*.

I clear my throat and stab a hunk of celery on to the end of my fork. 'La Roux here was only telling me the other day how much he admires hens,' I say.

'My,' Big mutters, 'how absolutely *fascinating*.'

Patch sniggers. I kick her under the table. She winces.

'I couldn't help wondering, La Roux,' she then suddenly pipes up (like the shrillest kind of cheap penny whistle), 'how it feels to be part of a white supremacist minority?'

La Roux stops chewing and frowns for a minute. 'Believe it or not,' he answers, after a short, slightly painful duration, 'I had absolutely no *inkling* that was the set up here. But I'm certain . . .' he smiles widely, 'that I'll get in to the swing of things once I'm fully adjusted.'

He takes another mouthful, looks up at the ceiling and chews on it piously. Patch emits a small, trumped growl, while under the table I feel that moist ginger victor push his bony knee even harder against mine. I try and shift sideways, but to no avail.

Feely, meanwhile, has begun staring again. This time Big notices. 'It's rude to stare, Feely,' he barks. 'I suggest you get on with eating.'

Feely dutifully picks up a spoon, scoops a mouthful of spinach onto it, pops it between his lips, knocks it back like a bitter pill and swallows it whole. The spinach goes two gentle rounds with his troublesome tonsils then picks a *real* fight with his unwelcoming oesophagus. The result? He starts choking.

Patch – the girl's on constant *standby* for this kind of drama – slaps his back with the flat of her hand. *Hard*. And that bastard

92

Four Year Old promptly coughs up this unobliging green nugget straight down and out and on to the table.

*Urgh.*

'How many times', Big asks, his voice suddenly sharp-bladed as a *Stanley*, 'are you expected to chew your food before swallowing?'

I open my mouth to answer but Big silences me. 'Not you, Medve. I'm asking Feely.'

Feely scratches his nose, rolls his eyes and doesn't utter a word, let alone a *number*.

'How many times, Feely?'

'Uh,' Feely stares at the recently expelled blob of spinach. 'Three hundred and fifty times,' he guesses.

'Thirty-six times,' Big says, 'is what dieticians generally recommend.'

He reaches out his hand, plucks the gobbet of spinach from the table-top, pulls down Feely's chin, pops it in, closes his mouth and says, 'Thirty-six times. Let's count together, shall we?'

He glances around the table. 'Shall we? La Roux? Medve? Patch? Shall we?'

Everybody nods, sullenly but *en masse*.

'Right, let's all take a mouthful . . .' He places a half-red-onion between his lips, smiling. We all do likewise, but *sans* smile.

'*And,*' he chews once, then speaks. 'One!' Chews a second time. 'Two!' A third time. 'Three!'

So it continues.

'*Swallow!*' he bellows, on thirty-six.

We all swallow. Then he takes a second random scoop of

something and starts right on over from scratch again (In truth, I don't think he's even really *enjoying* this pointless piece of power-play. It's as if he's cheerfully relating a dirty joke to a random stranger he just met at a party, only to suddenly discover, pre-filthy-punchline, that the man in question is a vicar. But he tells the joke anyway. He's in too *deep*, if you get my meaning).

Big's voice, as he counts, is harsh as wire wool, but his poor face is ashen, his eyes are bulging and his two cheeks are moist as Bobby Ewing's handshake. One to thirty-six. We follow, we swallow. And then, would you believe it, this undersized but extra-zealous human calculator ratchets himself up a *third* time over.

It can't last. And it doesn't. At formal chew number ninety-seven, Big stops, takes a huge, strangled breath, pushes his plate away – knocking the jug of lemon water flying – pulls himself heavily to his feet and storms from the room. I'm talking mid-count, mid-mouthful, mid-*everything*.

For a while nobody dares to swallow. Then La Roux puts his fork down, spits a mashed-up glob of something unspeakable on to his plate, and mournfully inspects his soaking lap.

'I feel a little nauseous,' he whispers.

'*Poor* Big,' Patch sighs, matter-of-factly, bone dry herself and already scooping up a brand new forkful, 'it's all the fault of that *damn* telegram.'

Feely sniffs, kicks his feet together and quietly watches the lemon liquid trickle in a waterfall from the slats to the floor, while (with exceptional stealth and surreptitiousness), just inches away on the opposite underside of that tiny table, La Roux silently places his only remaining dry four fingers and

94

thumb down so gently onto my soggy thigh that it's like a moth landing, then squeezes me there – once, twice – for a few brief seconds.

How do I react? I don't react. What do I do? I don't do *anything*. You see, I'm much too busy staring up and out of that old ship's porthole and fervently wishing – just for a moment – that I could cast myself off from this whole infuriatingly trying biological misalliance, straighten my jib, unfurl my sails, head straight for that true, blue horizon and float blissfully away.

Who do I think *I'm* kidding?

*Yeah?* And what if I happen to *like* his hand there, anyway?

Big, it later transpires, has stormed off to the mainland (so no prizes for guessing whose turn it was to do the dishes today). Luckily La Roux helps out with the post-lunch chores. Patch washes, he dries. I supervise with half an eye as I cut a very sulky Feely's fingernails, having promised faithfully to read him something cheery when this grim odyssey is over.

La Roux and Patch, I observe (above the white blotches of Feely's chronic calcium deficiency) are getting on like a house on fire. He has *subdued* her in some indefinable way (So they share the same landing: it was inevitable they'd grow *familiar*, if only on the basis of forced proximity, but what I'm seeing here is something quite *beyond* the ordinary).

As I quietly sit (literally transfixed by this two-faced rusted fox's well-honed Machiavellian spooning – *and* he's drying the cutlery! It's all *too* perfect!), I watch him effortlessly cementing Patch's easy affections with a most maddening new game he quickly devises.

Whenever she seems in danger of leaving the room for some random reason (to hang out a dishcloth or empty the rubbish), La Roux will suddenly bellow, '*Patch! No! Don't go!*' as though his heart will break if she even so much as *considers* withdrawing.

Every time he tries this gambit (and she's a *mobile* little monkey with an *exceptionally* weak bladder), the girl pauses, blushes, falters, then slowly starts cackling. She practically laps up the attention. It's all so *embarrassing*. (Not to mention galling; I've seen feral cats more sincere than this fucker.)

When they've finally got around to completing the dishes (with so much billing and cooing it gets to feeling like a bloody pigeon loft in that kitchen: I mean bullshit and feathers right up to the rafters), La Roux suddenly decides that he wants Patch to cut his hair.

He plumps himself down on a stool – just one place along from sulky Feely – and asks for the scissors.

'These are *nail* scissors,' I tell him, passing them over.

He completely ignores me (right, so I'm *Plague Girl* now, all of a sudden?) and gently entrusts the blades into Patch's keen, plump fingers.

'While you're cutting,' he tells her, 'I'll just sit back, relax, and listen in on Feely's story.'

He pats Feely on the shoulder. Feely grimaces (he's not fooled. He's still mistrustful, and he's *horribly* proprietorial about his fictions), then pitter-patters off to fetch his bean-bag. I set about trying to find the appropriate book, with the requisite amount of banging and swearing.

Patch, meanwhile (supremely oblivious), quietly discusses La Roux's *trichological* aspirations.

'I think you need it short at the sides but fluffy on top. That's the style of the moment. Do you know the pop star Terry Hall?' she asks. 'He's the stupid, blond one in Fun Boy Three?'

'I don't, actually, but here's my idea,' he tells her. 'You know how it is when someone catches a ringworm?'

She frowns, not quite getting it. 'You mean on their head? In their hair?'

He nods. 'Exactly. Let's do that, keeping the overall look and length much as it is currently, just cutting out a couple of bald circles in really unexpected places.'

Patch muses this over for a minute, in silence.

'Think you're up to it, technically?' La Roux asks.

Patch's serious face breaks into a wide smile. She repositions the scissors on her fingers. 'Hell,' she says firmly, 'just shut up and *watch* me.'

Feely quietly returns, having located his bean-bag. I show him the book. He smiles, plumps himself down and makes himself comfy as I flip through the pages, lounging casually up against the cobwebbed Aga.

'Okay,' I tell him, 'I can do you five paragraphs on the Kasuga Grand Shrine . . .' He winces. Not a particular favourite. 'Or a page and a half about the Art and Architecture of the Kofuku Temple . . .'

Feely waves his arm and closes his eyes languidly (he *knows* what he's here for). 'Just give me the deer,' he whispers.

'Fine,' I tell him, 'but I'll read it once only. That's the rule.' (This child's a devil for sordid repetitions.)

He nods, pulls in his paws and balls up completely, neatly tucking his mucky knees under his dirty ears.

La Roux raises his hand while Patch snips up a storm; hair flying everywhere. I glance over.

'What the fuck kind of children's story is this, anyway?' he asks.

I show him the cover. 'It's a book about the Japanese city of Nara. Feely's brother Barge used to read it to him when he was a baby. It's his favourite. He finds it extremely *calming*.'

La Roux scowls but says nothing. Feely opens one eye and shifts a little. I notice his disquiet and resolve – before his unusually restful demeanour can be further disrupted – to smartly commence with the reading.

'*The Deer of Nara*,' I begin softly.

'Deer?' La Roux mutters. 'In a *city*?'

I ignore him.

'*Shiro Chan, Queen of the deer of Nara*.' I glance up. 'That's the subtitle.'

La Roux sticks his hands under his opposite armpits (eclipsing his embroidered pony) and stares at me with a worryingly attentive air.

I continue, '"There are approximately one thousand deer in Nara Park. While the bucks proudly display their large antlers, the does gently tend to their fawns. One doe was born with a strange crown of white fur on the top of her head. She was very popular with all the tourists . . ."'

At this point, Feely – one eye still open – swallows down a huge gulp of ill-suppressed emotion (He knows what's coming). I pause briefly, to let it all sink in. La Roux's own eyes are slowly widening. I repeat the sentence, 'Yes, "one doe was born with a strange crown of white fur on the top of her head. She was very popular with all the tourists and they called her Shiro Chan. But after only a few short years of life, Shiro Chan was killed in a traffic accident. It would seem that a true beauty is fated to live a short life only, even among the deer."'

I squat down next to Feely. 'Want to see the picture?'

He lifts his head and peeks. 'The beautiful Shiro Chan . . .' He recites the caption automatically. '. . . Yes. I see her.'

I close the book. Feely collapses back, replete. La Roux blinks repeatedly, 'Is that *it*?'

I nod.

'And you say reading this book was your brother Barge's idea?'

I nod again.

'Is he some kind of maniac?'

I glare. 'Not that I'm aware of.'

'He's living on a kibbutz,' Patch intervenes, as if inadvertently determined to justify all La Roux's worst prejudices, 'in the Baltics. He's hoping to become a famous painter one day. He lost the tip of his tongue in a fight defending the honour of our oldest sister. It was terribly tragic. He needed twenty-seven stitches. Which is loads.'

'In his *tongue*?' La Roux is plainly appalled.

'Yup.'

'And is he a good painter?'

Patch snorts. 'Really *bad*. He's nuts about L. S. Lowry. He paints red houses. Industrial scenes. That kind of thing. With a palette knife. He *eschews* brushes. It's very messy. I've repeatedly told him my theory about how the real future of art is in cat paintings. Cats, flowers and cottages. That's what people prefer nowadays. Nobody in the eighties wants to be reminded of Britain's great industrial heritage. It's all terribly *passé*.'

'Cats?'

'I'm *telling* you.'

La Roux is silent for a minute, as if quietly thinking something over. 'Do you really, honestly believe, Medve,' he suddenly turns and asks me, 'that true beauty is fated to live a short life only, *even among the deer*?'

I glance down at Feely, somewhat cautiously, and hedge my bets. 'I can't say I know enough about deer to answer that question either way.'

La Roux shakes his head.

'Stop shaking,' Patch tells him, 'or you'll mess up your ring.'

'A *road traffic accident*,' La Roux repeats. 'It's plainly impractical to keep wild animals in a modern city. And to think I actually had the Japanese down as a sensible people.' He pauses. 'So let me see the picture of this crazy, white-headed doe for a minute . . .'

He puts out his hand. I pick up the book again and am just about to pass it over when Feely explodes from his bean-bag, snatches the book away from me, yells, 'How *dare* you make fun of Shiro Chan!' and then copiously wets himself where he stands. Before anyone can add anything, he hurtles – with all the speed and precision of a one-wheeled biplane attempting an emergency landing with a serious fuel leak – out of the kitchen.

La Roux shrugs, sighs and peers mournfully after him. 'I can't help thinking', he murmurs thoughtfully, 'how that poor, morbid child takes a little too much after his tiny father.'

Immediately after – as if nothing at all significant has happened – he starts telling a fascinated Patch, at length, about his troubled South African school-days (about the unflattering shorts he wore and the horrible haircuts, about the corporal punishment and the compulsory rugby. Oh, the eternal smarts of a *thousand* indignities!) while I slide around silently on the slippy tiles, do a spot of mopping, grab a fresh cloth, the bean-bag, a Pomfret cake, and then skid grimly off to try and tackle the too-tender, one-wheeled, wet-bellied plane-wreck of little Feely.

Just four brief years old, dear Reader, and *my*, what a tangle.

## 11

*So they give you the regulation pep-talk, render you horizontal, stick these blessed little pins in your ears and then bugger off for half an hour. At first there's a burning and your whole face turns scarlet. Then there's a nasty, queasy interlude. Then an overwhelming taste of metal (like licking a newly sharpened knife, or getting a filling, or chewing down hard on silver foil).*

*After fifteen minutes – I'm staring listlessly up at the ceiling all the while – the acupuncturist returns briefly to give the pins a little twizzle. He peers down at my ears with an expression of intense satisfaction. 'I think everything's in order,' he tells me (obviously ludicrously impressed by his own sterling efficiency), then scarpers off again with all the sharp-heeled and officious dispatch of Alice's White Rabbit.*

*Some pins hurt much more than others when he moves them. I think they're in deeper. There are eight of them in total: seven in the left ear, one in the right. As he touches them I bite my tongue, clench my fists and try my damnedest not to whimper.*

*As he's leaving me again I turn my head slightly – but very carefully, anxious not to knock the pins into the pale, crochet-covered counterpane – and say, 'By the way, I really like your dog picture . . .'*

*I indicate towards the bedside table, where, taking pride of place, is a black-and-white photo of an unappealing cross-breed: tongue out, head cocked, salivating regally. Impeccably framed. A visibly*

*ancient thing but much beloved. A reproduction. Blown up.*
*Touched up. But in terrible condition.*

*I don't know if this evasive acupuncturist hears me. If he does, he*
*doesn't trouble himself to answer.*

I have no *business* dreaming about Jack Henry Abbott. Yet
suddenly this crazy Yank celebrity killer is marching around
like an armed guard inside my night-times. He's lecturing me,
at length, about Marx and inequality and *perception*. He's rant-
ing and raving and speaking in *italics*.

Sometimes they drug him and his words are blurred. At
these times he drones on endlessly about *hope* and *despair* and
*human weakness*. Sometimes he's pacing silently (These are the
worst times. His silence is *remorseless*). Sometimes he's writing
poetry. He flirts with haiku: three lines, seventeen syllables.
He says he actively enjoys the *restriction*, the *containment* of this
particular art form. He relishes it. He finds it *ironic*.

Yeah, Jack Henry. Ha fucking *ha*.

Sometimes he starves himself. He's still extremely angry. In
fact he's *livid* – even though I keep trying to tell him this is *my*
dream and he's as free as a bird in it. *Free*. Paroled. Friday the
fifth. The very same day on which (I idly mention) that screw-
ball South African first set his two promiscuously cheesy feet
on our innocent part-island.

But this professional, hard-edged, handcuffed misan-
thropist isn't even *remotely* interested in the stuff I'm telling
him. He says he has a whole fifty-four card *pack* of his own
problems to deal with.

*You're free, you lucky fucker. Get out of my damn head!*

But he won't go. It's as if he's waiting for something. Just squatting angrily in a corner, like he's taking a *dump*, muttering and scowling and stewing and staring.

Holy *Lamb*! My unconscious is running me bloody *ragged*.

I'm hanging around aimlessly, waiting for Big to dawdle home. It's already a ridiculous hour: too late to be night, too early to be morning. I guess I feel it's my daughterly duty (as his oldest remaining nest-bound offspring – I'm his rock, I'm his strength, I'm his *staff*, I tell you) to keep a keen eye out for his general well-being.

Waking. Dreaming. Book on my lap (no prizes for fingering the criminal who wrote it), propped up in a wicker chair and wrapped in a blanket. No light, just the moon through my domed-glass ceiling. No sound, just the wicker creaking and the stained tiles rattling.

Jack Henry is telling me about his plans to escape. He got out once (1971, if I remember correctly) for an outrageously cheeky six-week vacation. Lay low in a hotel room in Ontario, Canada. And at night – this is the cruellest irony – he dreamed he was back in the hole, back in prison, back in solitary: just pacing and pacing and endlessly pacing.

After six short weeks they caught him and banged him up again.

Born in Michigan: an unwanted baby. Enjoyed a bad run of foster accommodation. *Shunted* from place to place like an empty fairground dodgem. Turned rotten aged nine. Spent a spell in juvenile detention. Went back at twelve, followed by six long years in some crazy sub-military institution.

Free for a short span at eighteen – age of *consent* I believe they call it. Issued a cheque against insufficient funds. Was arrested. At which point, at long last, the Big Boys – the real retributionary *players* – finally got their grubby hands on him (or that's how he's telling it).

Killed a man in prison. *Self-defence*, he hollers. And that was the end. That was when they buried him. Except he had a sister. And a sympathetic bookshop. Who sent him just the kind of stuff he needed to survive it . . .

Big tomes, slim volumes, hardbacks, softbacks. History, philosophy, politics. Jack Henry got self-educated. Slowly lost his sense of humour. Started a correspondence with famous writer Norman Mailer (then seriously *obsessed* by legendary death row prisoner/martyr – depending on how you look at it – Gary Gilmore).

Abbott picked him up, when he needed it, on points of ideological and factual accuracy. I mean he was an *insider*, wasn't he? He was the man they called The Professor.

Nobody, but *nobody*, fucked with him.

Footsteps on the parquet. At first I think it's Big back home (but the more I mull it over, the more I realize the tide's all *wrong* for crossing by foot at this particular hour). Through the foyer, the dining-room, out on to the balcony, then back in again, slowly, down the smooth loop of stairs and into the kitchen.

This oddly aimless and arbitrary wandering continues for what feels like an eternity . . . Back up the stairs, into the snooker room, the foyer, a lengthy pause in front of the part-draped statue of Diana, some utterly inexplicable *scratching*.

Then finally (and I'm hardly breathing at this stage), a gradual, almost *nervy* materialization in my doorway. Eight or nine feet away. He hesitates, then shuffles forward like he's in shackles. The moonlight shines down on him.

La Roux, in his nightwear: a pair of undersized pyjamas, flapping like mainsails above his ankles. And he has something with him, by his heels, in the darkness. I slowly start breathing again. '*La Roux!*' I chastize him in an anxious whisper. 'Are you trying to scare the living *shit* out of me?'

He doesn't answer. He turns and shuffles across the Peacock Lounge, running his hand along the shiny-tiled cocktail bar. He carefully avoids my mattress and bedding. The darker, smudgy creature follows, like a dog, a short distance behind him.

He pauses, briefly (obscured by a parlour palm). I hear some furtive scuffling followed by a gentle tinkle. I think he may well be pissing in the empty fountain.

'La *Roux*! What the *fuck* are you doing?'

I speak louder this time and clamber to my feet. He strolls around the fountain and directly towards me.

'I'm walking the dog,' he answers calmly.

His voice is a dull monotone, and when he speaks it's into the air directly to the left of where I'm standing.

'Did you say *dog*?'

'*Spookie*. Little Spookie. Little ghost. Our tiny puppy.'

And now he's talking like a baby.

'What's the matter with you?'

He shakes his head, frowning. 'You never liked the dog, did you, Gavin? Not after you found it licking me. But there really was nothing wrong with it. It was simply a matter of two lost souls coming together and . . .' he thinks for a moment, '. . . and *comforting* one another.'

'It's Medve, you moron.' I wave my hand at him. He doesn't blink or react. This skinny, flimsy-pyjamaed ginger boy is plainly sleepwalking. I think he believes I'm his *brother* or someone. I'm not entirely certain but I'm pretty sure I remember him mentioning a single male sibling previously. Slightly older than him. One or two years, maybe?

'My brother,' he explains slowly (thereby instantly confirming my suspicions) and speaking like he's remembering a difficult piece of calculus, or a poem, or a biblical quotation, 'got bitten by a crocodile in a southern tributary of the great Okovango River . . .'

I'm about to talk but he interrupts me.

'On patrol,' he says suddenly. 'On the Angolan border. The Caprivi Strip,' he shudders, 'in Namibia.'

Then he turns and whistles, over his shoulder, very softly.

'Was he badly hurt?'

'Huh?' he turns back again, plainly irritated.

'Your brother. Was he hurt? Did it kill him?'

He laughs drily.

'Why are you laughing?'

'He was fine. It was a *dare*. Those were the kinds of things we did back then. You know, just to pass the time when we weren't murdering the boys from SWAPO or raping their women in the outlying villages . . .'

He sighs. 'War can be very boring . . .' He pauses, ominously. 'And that's always when the truly *bad* things start to happen . . .'

His breathing deepens.

'What were you doing in Namibia?' I ask gently (if *only* I'd followed Patch's reading itinerary – then, at least, all this strategic babble wouldn't sound like utter *Greek* to me).

'I was conscripted. I was *fighting* . . .' he cackles hollowly, then shakes his head. 'I don't know what the *fuck* I was doing . . . But when they tried to give me a gun . . .'

He puts out his hands as if to protect himself from something.

'What's wrong?'

'I said, "If you give me a gun I'll kill you with it." So they compromised and made me a medic instead.'

He laughs again, but his mouth is turning down at its corners.

'Did you mean it?'

La Roux scratches his head, confusedly, 'Mean *what* . . .?' he thinks for a moment. 'That I'd kill them? Of course not. I could never . . . That was the whole *point*, stupid.'

He pauses, keeping his hands in his hair. 'In the sands of the Namib, the desert children are nannied by dogs. They lick their arses clean when they've finished shitting. They keep them spotless. It's always happened. There's nothing wrong with it.'

I remain silent.

'There's nothing *wrong* with it,' he mutters defensively. 'I *know* what you're thinking. I know. And how after you caught me you could never really bear to look at me again. Not properly. Only sideways. And disapproving. Just like the rest of them. Then the dog gave me ringworm. And you said it was God punishing me for being so completely fucking *disgusting*.'

He continues to touch his scalp. 'Do you feel the rings? I feel them.' He sighs, 'Spookie would lick them better. We caught lizards in the garden together right up until the day he died. July 15th, 1977. From tick-bite fever.'

We are both silent for a while.

'I have to get up early in the morning,' he suddenly informs me. Then he taps his leg, as if calling a dog to heel, and begins walking again, slowly, towards the door. Which is precisely when I'm consumed by a sudden, heart-stopping chill, because that small, dark thing I'd noticed previously is back again, and resolutely trailing in his wake like a clumsy shadow.

I stare a little harder. Then I distinguish this curious creature's parameters. Not a ghost dog at all, but a huge clump of tangled wool, strung around his right ankle, with Big's best-beloved crochet odds-and-ends bag bumping and dragging just a short distance behind it.

Sweet Lord *above*, what a fucking *wind*-up.

Big returns an hour later. I'm fast asleep in bed by then, but he creeps in on boot-heavy legs to check up on me (I mean, what does he *imagine* I might be doing?). I open my eyes to see his tiny torso retreating apologetically.

'Big,' I whisper.

He peers over his shoulder. 'Go back to sleep.'

I sit up. 'Where did you get to?'

'I just went walking.'

'Where did you end up?'

'Salcombe. In a pub.'

Even doze-dazed I'm astonished by this revelation. Big is no barfly (he doesn't have it *in* him, either socially *or* digestively speaking). My slow mind instantly starts churning: are things really much worse between him and Mo than I'd initially imagined?

'Did you *drink* anything?' I ask, secretly moved by his manly bravura.

'Tomato juice with *Worcestershire Sauce*.' He rubs his stomach. 'And I'm paying for it already, actually.'

I deflate internally. 'And the route? Did you go the Churchstow–Marlborough way?' (Okay, so I'm a girl *obsessed* by orientation. No law against that, is there?)

He chuckles. 'What is this? Twenty questions? I took the small roads. I simply *meandered*. Uh . . .' He counts the villages off on his fingers, 'Bigbury, Buckland, Outer Hope . . .'

'Really?' I suddenly interrupt him. 'And how was that?'

He frowns. 'Pardon me?'

'Outer Hope. How was it?'

'Smallish. Couple of pubs. Nothing fancy. In fact . . .'

'What?'

He pauses for a moment. 'I phoned your mother while I was there. From the phone booth. It was . . .' There's a smile in his voice but I can't really clock his exact expression, 'a rather *bad* connection.'

'Oh.' I'm suddenly anxious – don't ask me why – 'And how was she?'

He shrugs. 'Full of it. As ever. Told me how Poodle's been staying with her for a while. Stopped working for Donovan Healy about three weeks ago, and has severed the connection for good, it seems. Mo said she was very obdurate – no, *mulish* – about the whole thing.'

'Really?' I cluck tartly. 'No surprises there, then.'

He ignores me. 'She was in hospital in Denver for a few days. Nothing too serious. Just . . . uh . . .' he grapples for the word, 'something *cosmetic*.'

His voice sounds disapproving. 'And she'll probably be coming home soon, to recuperate properly, but only if we really try and play our cards right. As a *family*, I mean.'

There's a warning tone in his voice which I don't *quite* appreciate.

'Okay.'

I lie down again (yes of *course* I'm absolutely charmed and delighted and ecstatic and everything).

'Well,' he says eventually, clearly disturbed by my mono-syllabic reaction, 'I'll be seeing you in the morning.'

I close my eyes. 'It *is* morning, stupid.'

He turns to go. 'Okay, *smart-arse*,' he mutters, tip-toeing off and closing the door gently behind him, 'there's no need to get all flip and sassy with me.'

## 12

Five a.m. My fickle eyes (having been as bright as a Chelsea Pensioner's buttons all the dark night long) would seem to have chosen this hugely inauspicious time to self-seal by way of a glutinous *slew* of crusty secretions. It's as if my upper and lower lashes have all been individually crisp-crumbed by the illusory fingers of a phantasmagorical chef, and then slowly and painstakingly golden-battered together. It's *putrid*.

I rub away the worst of it as I slam out of the hotel and stagger resolutely downhill to meet with Black Jack for our somewhat untimely fishing assignation.

The sun has already risen in the east like an undercooked ivory-coloured muffin. The gulls swoon above me, full of early morning zeal, bleating like spring lambs and experimenting on a riotous helter-skelter of wind currents. Hovvering, swooping, diving.

Because it's fairly breezy, I yank my lilac-coloured crochet cardigan a little tighter around me, shove up my shoulders, curse a few times and readjust my unwieldy fishing equipment (all ancient stuff, but *exceptionally* hardy, passed down by Mo's great uncle who game-kept in the Scottish Highlands before volunteering for that worthy but – in his own case – rather *tragic* Spanish Civil War business).

I have an emergency banana stuffed into my woolly pocket, for energy. And frankly, I am most *miserably* in need of it –

feeling as I do, at that precise moment, about as well-worn and washed-out as a busy whore's best knickers – but I hold off peeling and devouring it (time is of the essence) and plod bravely onwards, my stomach growling, all the while, like a territorial Alsatian.

On approaching the jetty – the swollen tide is already quietly contemplating the possibility of rushing out again – something wholly unexpected makes me stop, start violently and widen my heavy, sleep-encrusted eyes to fuller than their full capacity.

For there, large as Lucifer, a mere thirty yards or so ahead of me, stands that horrid, blackguard, hell-hound *La Roux*, lounging against the huge wheel of the sea tractor (fully balaclavaed), looking lively as a sharp south-westerly (the *bastard*) and deep in cheery conversation with Jack the Skipper.

He is holding something. As I draw closer I see it is a ball of dough, but bright yellow, which he is gently massaging in the palm of his hand to (as he expresses it) 'maintain its texture'. Jack is staring at this ball with great attention, all previous difficulties between the two of them now plainly forgotten. (How the hell does he *do* it? This man is more rank and slippery than a bed of oysters. He could give the Reverend Jim Jones a run for his money. They should seriously consider funding research into his human-management techniques for the United Nations.)

As I draw closer I am able to decipher certain choice segments of his shameless patter. It turns out that this unappetizing yellow muck is an all-but *legendary* South African fishbait (Yeah. Believe that and you'll believe *anything*). Phenomenal stuff, La Roux's telling him, both for fresh *and* for saltwater fishing. Nothing too fancy either, just a rough-and-ready mixture of dough and cheese and curry powder. In all the right proportions, obviously.

After perusing this wonderbait at some length, sniffing it, squeezing it and touching it with the tip of his tongue, Black Jack finally gets around to apprehending my arrival, and affords me the kind of minutely surprised look you might give a traditionally attired Elizabethan princess who appears unannounced and noisily demanding to join a clutch of horny-handed men of toil in the pursuit of something manly.

I point to La Roux. 'What the hell is *he* doing here?'

Jack shows me the bait, almost sniggering. 'Have you *seen* this stuff? La Roux says fish'll bite off the hook for it.'

I take a closer look at this wondrous concoction. It seems vaguely familiar. It *reminds* me of something.

'Nice tackle, Medve,' La Roux observes benevolently, staring at my breasts, his eyes twinkling.

'Up your arse,' I mutter, clumping gracelessly across the wooden landing bay, climbing carefully on board the boat and hoping against hope – perhaps rather naïvely under the circumstances – that we'll be leaving the quisling South African behind us.

The boat is nothing fancy. A small rower with a smoky outboard motor. Seats two comfortably. It's a squeeze for three. La Roux – suddenly bedecked in a stinky life-jacket which reeks of perished rubber – springs on board (from whence does this man derive his crazy energy?) and rocks me green-gilled with a frenzied bout of horribly inexpert clambering.

I observe that he has his beloved twig with him, on the tip of which he has affixed a length of wool threaded with a small, bent, darning needle. And he absolutely *insists* on sitting at my end, right in the nose of the boat, like a preposterously over-sized figurehead, with his devilishly bony spine knocking repeatedly into mine every time the boat jerks or a random wave rocks us unexpectedly.

The sea is slightly choppy to start off with, but thankfully it calms down after twenty minutes. Jack drops anchor approximately half a mile out into the bay. It's getting warmer. The wind is dropping. It's pretty much *perfect* fishing weather.

I bait my hook, check my reel, cast off – nothing too spectacular to begin with – and contentedly watch my fly bobbing among the gentle waves. Jack does likewise.

La Roux, having spent the duration hawking into the water, and trying (but failing) to encourage Jack to do the same on a competitive basis, eventually abandons this game when I spit something green and grievous at *least* five metres into the deep blue distance. He suddenly gazes up dreamily into the high clouds above him and casually pretends he hasn't noticed.

Eventually he affixes a huge chunk of wonderbait to his ridiculous needle and dips it in over the side. From the rear he resembles a lacklustre rubber gnome with disturbing paramilitary tendencies.

At long last, for the first (and unfortunately the final) time during our short voyage, he voluntarily observes the habitual meditative silence of the serious fisherperson.

I use this brief and blissful hiatus to pull out my banana and peel it. La Roux's head suddenly whips around like a hungry gull's (I'm talking 180 degrees, *minimum*). 'What *is* that?' he asks.

I frown. 'What does it *look* like? It's a fucking banana.'

'May I have some?'

'No.'

'Oh, come on.'

'No.'

'Oh, come *on*.'

*'No!'*

'But I'm *starving*.'

'La Roux, you're *killing* me.' I bite off half the fruit in a single mouthful and then viciously swallow it.

'My God, I can't believe you just did that.'

*'Believe.'*

I consume the second half just as spiritedly – 'Yum!' – and toss the skin overboard.

La Roux peers down into the water to watch it sinking. Then he turns to stare at Jack. 'Do you have anything worth eating at your end, Jack?' he enquires ingratiatingly. Jack is manhandling a lugworm. He glances up, hardly listening. 'Uh . . . no. Nothing.'

'He only has lugworms,' I interject helpfully.

*'Lug*worms?' La Roux repeats the name with interest. 'Okay,' he says, 'pass one over.'

Jack appears not to hear him. But I won't miss this opportunity.

'Jack,' I say firmly. 'Lugworm.'

A deeply preoccupied Jack distractedly hands me his tupperware tub. Inside it, fifteen lugworms squirm delightfully, each of them that delicious trademark blood-mud-red colour. I pop in my fingers and pull one out.

'Here you go.' I proffer it to La Roux.

He inspects the gyrating worm for a few brief moments, rolls up his balaclava, takes it from me (this particular prime specimen is a good four inches) and tosses it into his mouth. Two quick chews and a big swallow follow.

I emit a little scream (yes, I *know* it's beneath me to behave so *girlishly*, even if I *am* a girl of the giant variety). Jack glances over. 'Have you hooked something?'

'Uh. No. La Roux just ate a lugworm,' I explain sheepishly.

The Worm Eater is already readjusting his balaclava. Jack looks nonplussed. 'If I'd known you were that desperate,' he says, reaching into his jacket pocket, 'I'd've given you an Iced Gem.'

La Roux's head snaps around again. 'What was that?' he asks, his back instantly straightening.

'An Iced Gem,' Jack repeats, holding up a small packet of this obscure miniature-multi-coloured-icing-topped-biscuit-based delicacy.

On espying these alien English sweetmeats, La Roux begins wriggling like a puppy.

'Oh yes,' he says, 'I'll certainly be willing to try one of those.'

'Believe it or not,' Jack informs me (ignoring the eager La Roux with most magnificent aplomb), 'I like to use these things to attract tiddlers. For some strange reason they seem to have a real *appetite* for them.'

He pulls open the small packet and tosses a large handful into the water. La Roux howls like a wounded wolf.

As if only just apprehending La Roux's interest, Jack pulls out a couple extra and hurls them his way. In his frenzy to catch them La Roux elbows me in both the ear and the shoulder. I complain vociferously, but to no avail. La Roux catches one, but the second lands in the water. Even so, he holds his tiny prize in the palm of his hand and stares at it lovingly. '*Iced Gem*,' he repeats, and stares some more.

My eyes return firmly to my gently bobbing fly, while behind me a sudden ecstatic crunching commences. Five quiet seconds pass. Jack reels in his line.

'I need another *Iced Gem*!' La Roux suddenly bellows. 'Give them to me!'

I turn on him. 'Would you actually mind *shutting bloody up* for a single minute? You're scaring the fish away with all that racket.'

'I *need* an *Iced Gem*!' La Roux shouts. 'I just love them. I've fallen in love with them. Give me another. *Give me another Iced Gem*. Give one to *meeeeee*.'

Jack completely ignores him (He seems to have perfected this capability). He pushes a worm on to his hook and casts it out again.

'*Iced Gem*!' La Roux yells.

I turn to Jack. 'For God's sake, I can't stand it. Please do us both a favour and just *give* him one.'

Jack points. 'See. Over there . . .'

I wincingly (the sheer volume of La Roux's expostulations is simply *deafening*) follow the line of his finger. A short distance away an isolated but still-floating Iced Gem is being consumed by something scaly.

'I *told* you they loved them.'

Jack shoves his hand once again into the open packet and casts a few more out to sea.

'*No!*' La Roux howls.

Jack smiles (he can't *help* himself), puts the packet down onto the bench beside him and reels in his line a little. My fly bobs. I yank up the rod and also start reeling. Jack notices. 'A bite?' he asks encouragingly.

'Can't quite tell as yet . . .' I continue reeling, breathing heavily.

During this brief moment of fisherly distraction, La Roux – without any kind of warning – suddenly hurls himself across the boat towards the packet of Iced Gems, shoving me discourteously aside in the process.

I almost topple overboard. The whole boat rocks wildly. But Jack's much too quick for him, and snatches the Gems – or most of them – out of harm's way before La Roux's frantically lunging hands are able to grab a firm hold. Three tip on to the mucky floor and La Roux manages to herd them together. Then (like an electric eel which has recently emerged from its coral hunting hidey-hole) he rapidly retreats again.

A further, elongated bout of ecstatic crunching follows. Whatever was once on my line has now slipped off it. I reel in, cursing darkly, and rebait. 'You know what?' I gurgle over my shoulder. 'You are worse than a bloody animal. You are an absolute *fucking* liability.'

'Ah, fuck you back,' La Roux mutters, still crunching enthusiastically, his birdy-eyes peering greedily at Jack over the length of the boat again.

'He's like a starling,' Jack says, glancing over and (would you *believe* this?) smiling indulgently. 'Just *look* at him. Just look at those tiny, sharp eyes. A starling.'

La Roux pauses mid-crunch. 'What's a starling?'

'A greasy little brown bird. Very *noisy*,' I tell him coldly.

Jack nods his agreement, then, 'Ooops,' he expostulates, focusing forward, 'something's nibbling.'

It's at this point that the lucky *swine* casually bags a three-pound mackerel. No fuss. No rigmarole. No unmanly hassle. I watch in awe while he reels it in and then enviously eyeball his prodigious catch as he proudly unhooks it.

'They're only not biting my end,' I tell him sulkily, 'because of this *noisy bastard* here.' I thumb contemptuously towards La Roux.

'I'm so *hungry*, so terribly *hungry*,' La Roux is muttering. 'How long before we can head back home again?' (We've been in the boat, at this stage, all of thirty minutes.)

Jack deftly concusses his catch on the edge of the vessel. 'Couple more hours,' he answers casually. A powerful silence ensues from La Roux's end as he digests this terrible revelation.

'Two *hours*?' he gasps finally, his voice hollow with horror.

'Approximately,' Jack says.

'But how will I *survive* it?' La Roux bellows.

'By catching some fish like you're supposed to,' Jack tells him, 'that's how.'

It is at this awful juncture that La Roux suddenly notices that he has lost his beloved twig (I fear it fell into the water during his struggle for the Iced Gem packet. And maybe I *helped* it, God forgive me). He is devastated.

'I can't believe I lost my twig,' he keeps saying. 'I just *can't* believe I lost it.'

I cast out again, firmly resolving to simply ignore him. After a brief two minute silence during which time La Roux is noisily consuming the remainder of his sticky yellow ball of wonder-bait, his voice pipes up again. 'I need protein,' he says determinedly. 'Bring me the lugworms. Just pass the tub over.'

'No,' I growl, 'we're *fishing* with them.'

'Then give me an Iced Gem,' he wheedles.

'No.'

'You know what?' Jack says, as if suddenly awakening from a temporary reverie.

'No, what?' La Roux answers.

'It's only mentioning starlings earlier that made me think of it . . .'

I drag my eyes from my fly and turn to look at him. 'Made you think of what?'

'The parliament,' he says grandly. 'We have one locally. Have you ever seen it?'

I shake my head. 'Parliament? Nope. I've never even *heard* of it.'

'Me neither,' La Roux interjects.

'Well,' Jack expands, 'a parliament of starlings happens at sunset. But only in certain places and especially at certain times of year. They flock together – and I mean literally in their thousands – and do all this astonishingly acrobatic fly-ing, in formation. It's a really amazing sight. Definitely worth seeing.'

I'm immediately fascinated by this phenomenon. 'Wow. That sounds intoxicating.'

'You're telling me,' Jack agrees smugly.

Suddenly, and without *any* prior warning, La Roux (as if inspired by what Jack has been saying) starts to sing some-thing in the most offensively smarmy wail I have ever yet heard. He has a terrible voice. At once strong *and* weedy. I turn towards him. 'La *Roux*,' I say firmly (but calmly), ' I want you to *stop* doing that right now.'

He stops. 'Doing what?' he asks.

'I want you to stop singing that insufferable shit right this instant.'

'It's Andrew Lloyd-*Webber*,' he tells me (as if astonished by my ignorance). 'It's *Joseph and his Amazing Technicolor Dreamcoat*.'

'So?'

'*Joseph*, I tell you.'

'So?'

'It's the song Joseph sings when he's been forcibly kept by Herod's men against his will.'

'*So*?'

'You mean to tell me,' he pauses in horror, 'that you have never even seen *Joseph*?'

'No,' I echo blankly, 'I have never even seen it.'

La Roux's eyes bulge through his balaclava.

'I went and saw it in London a few years back, actually,' Jack intervenes, almost apologetically, 'but I can't say I entirely recognized it from what you were just singing.'

'Oh, come on.'

Jack shrugs. 'Sorry.'

'Oh, come *on*.'

Jack merely smiles.

'As it happens,' La Roux tells him, 'I personally *own* the original English Lloyd-Webber version on record. But in truth my favourite recording is the all-South-African-cast one. I went to see it in Johannesburg when I was seventeen. It featured the wonderful South African singer Bruce Millar as Joseph. I don't know if you've ever heard of him over here?'

Jack shakes his head. 'Not that I can recall.'

'Well,' La Roux continues determinedly, 'I would happily

bet a considerable amount of money that Bruce was probably the best Joseph in *any* production.'

Jack says nothing (He seems to have no particular feelings either way on this subject, and why *should* he?).

'The South African version had some minor differences to the English version,' La Roux continues, 'but they were all *good* differences in my opinion. They were *improvements*.'

Jack continues fishing in silence for a while and then he suddenly says, 'How can you be *sure* of that? You didn't even see the English version. Or any others, for that matter.'

La Roux (plainly delighted at having finally provoked some opposition, no matter how half-hearted) instantly jumps onto his high-horse and straddles it like a pincer-kneed professional. 'That's hardly the point,' he says. 'In my experience of musical theatre – which is extensive because we have a real *passion* for it in South Africa – I have never seen an actor so well cast for a role as Bruce was for *Joseph*.'

'But you didn't even *see* the English *Joseph*,' Jack counters dogmatically.

'I heard him on record and that was enough for me. He was useless. In fact he was *embarrassing*.'

Jack immediately takes offence at La Roux's harsh and fatuous criticisms. He indignantly draws himself up to his full height. 'He certainly wasn't useless when I saw him.'

'Well, he was useless on record. And Bruce was *great* recorded. That must mean something.'

Jack snorts derisively. 'I'm afraid I simply can't agree with you. A recording is a very different kettle of fish *indeed* from a live performance. Someone could easily perform live brilliantly and then record badly. It happens.'

'Fine,' La Roux concedes, 'but if you're such an admirer of his talents, how about telling me the actual *name* of the actor who played the English *Joseph*?'

Jack thinks hard for a minute. 'I can't honestly say I remember. All I can recollect is the fine performance he gave. I don't believe he was especially famous. I can't even recall having seen him in anything before or since . . .'

'But doesn't that *tell* you something?' La Roux expostulates victoriously. 'He performed in *Joseph* and then he sank without a trace. You *never heard of him again*. Listen to yourself! It's so *easy*. It's like snatching candy from a little baby.'

'No. I said *I'd* never heard of him since. That doesn't mean he didn't have a perfectly respectable career after. I just don't happen to follow the world of musical theatre as closely as . . .'

'*Enough!*' I bellow. 'What the heck is *wrong* with the two of you? That is *it*. If I hear another fucking *word* about *Joseph* I am going to kill somebody. I am *fishing*. Don't you know what that *means*? It's a *spiritual* experience. It's a kind of *devotion*. I need some peace and bloody *quiet!*'

Both men turn and stare at me with expressions of surprised incomprehension, as if my sudden show of bile is *entirely* disproportionate to the net irritation caused.

'Fine then,' Jack eventually mutters. 'Very sorry, I'm sure.'

He turns his back on us and reels in his line. As soon as he's not watching I poke a stiff finger into La Roux's spine (he yelps like a kitten). 'I *know* what you're doing,' I whisper ferociously, 'and you'll live to regret it if you carry on. Just shut the *fuck* up and stop driving me *crazy*.'

La Roux leans back a way and stares at me indignantly. 'Well get a load of you, Miss High and Mighty!' he exclaims.

'As far as I am aware,' he continues haughtily, 'you have absolutely no reason to believe my voice isn't actually deeply *alluring* to fish. In fact, you have no logical or scientific basis for thinking fish aren't actively *attracted* to my singing.'

'La Roux, just put a bloody *sock* in it,' I hiss.

I return to my rod. A mere five short seconds later, La Roux cheerfully commences whistling the overture to *Joseph and the Amazing Technicolor Dreamcoat* (the English version, naturally, to garner support from his Lloyd-Webber ally), then calmly proceeds to perform it in full. With a whole *infuriating* variety of embellishments.

Straight after the overture comes the first vocal number. And it is exactly half-way through his hyper-energetic performance of this song (during which the narrator kindly sets the BC scene) that I finally decide to throw my first punch.

Thereafter, things get *really* ugly.

When we arrive back at the island (a tumultuous twenty soggy, splashy, salty, sweaty minutes later), knuckles have been bitten, bruises have blossomed on lips and on backs-of-heads, blood has been drawn.

Jack clambers out first, ties up the boat, then turns and peers down at me.

'Is he still breathing?' he asks anxiously.

I peruse La Roux at my leisure. 'Of course he is. Can't you see his chest moving?'

'But did you really have to sit on his face *all* the way home?' Jack persists.

I smile, brightly. 'Come on, Jack, I gave him fair warning.

When I sat astride his chest he still *persisted* in whistling. In my book that's a declaration of war and at that point I was actively *obliged* to take the appropriate action. There *was* no alternative.'

Jack still doesn't look convinced. 'For heaven's sake,' I tell him, 'this man has had six months training in the South African armed forces. He's seen military action. I am a sixteen-year-old girl with a short fuse. It's hardly unfair competition.'

La Roux kicks out his right leg, furiously. Jack shrugs, rescues his mackerel and quickly makes off with it. As I watch him retreating, I take a good, deep breath, clench my buttocks one last time and then rise from that boat like a tall, teen, phoenix.

Unrepentant, ruddy-cheeked and *righteous*.

Yeah, *Buster*. That's me.

## 13

Talk about one *helluva* lousy and unproductive fishing expe-
dition. When I finally arrive home again (it's seven a.m.
already – I mean, the day's literally *over*), completely fish-free
and horribly groin-grazed (you honestly think he let me sit on
his face for quarter of an hour without champing at my genital region like an avenging two-humped camel?) I spend a fair
old while digging out and then trowelling half a bottle of Ger-
molene on to my assorted cuts and grazes.

My lower lip – I mutely observe in the bathroom mirror – is
fatter than a Christmas-week turkey and redder and *moister*
than a half-pint jug of cranberry jelly.

La Roux (very sensibly) lies low until way after eleven,
when I eventually catch a glimpse of him outside on the balcony, struggling to make his creepy peace with Feely (This
man's an emotional *juggler*. If he's out of favour in one place
he's bound to be energetically ingratiating himself in another).

After the awful Shiro Chan drama I'm astonished the loose-
bladdered little one will even *look* at him again, let alone
actively *welcome* his clumsy advances. But look he will, and
welcome he does (which I guess speaks volumes about the
natural, heedless *folly* of Human Nature; or maybe it's just my
small brother the *masochist* voluntarily offering his other
cheek in the secret anticipation of yet a further slapping).

Everything falls into place, though, when I finally discover *how* it is that La Roux's aiming to re-enter the Leaking Sprout's good graces. Not with Pomfret cakes or gentle kisses or games of Snap or Snakes and Ladders. No. He earns his forgiveness by dint of teaching him the complex and much-vaunted technique of burp-speaking (i.e. to speak coherent sentences in the guise of an extended belch).

This is, without doubt, just the kind of knack any well-adjusted whippersnapper might happily offer up his milk teeth for. Where, after all – I overhear La Roux asking rhetorically – is any real man *without* such a talent when participating in a riotous rugby club dinner, a bachelor party or a five-hour-long car journey?

Where? He wants to know *where*? Whatever happened to lighting farts, or hiring strippers or experimenting with depilatory cream or inhaling a reliably noxious cocktail of correction fluid, nail polish and paint thinners? (Is it just me or is the world really changing far too fast this half of the century?)

The secret to burp-speaking effectively – it turns out – lies in creating a syncopated rhythm of breathing and swallowing. It takes some doing. Although you wouldn't know it, to watch La Roux in action (demonstrating, experimenting, encouraging, enjoying), since he does it all so *naturally*; to the extent that I'm honestly starting to doubt whether English truly *is* his first language.

Indeed, to see this ginger gentleman valiantly burping is to observe true *indigestive* craftsmanship at it's absolute zenith. He can even recite the Twenty-third Psalm in belches with no artificial breaks or pauses. And he makes it look *effortless*.

Downstairs in the kitchen, meanwhile, poor Patch has been

thrown into a sudden confusion by the unexplained disappearance of her carefully pre-prepared lunch menu (spicy Moroccan Curry Balls, to you).

The oil smokes mournfully in the pan as she stares fixedly into the well-pilfered refrigerator and mutters, 'I'm *certain* I made twelve of those pesky things. Now there's only seven left, and two of *those* look partially regurgitated.'

(They actually say Agatha Christie was a regular visitor to these parts in the 1930s, and frankly, on the basis of what I've witnessed today, is it really any wonder? I mean, talk about a scintillating culinary-based art-deco murder-mystery in the making.)

Lunch is at one, formally, by which time La Roux has developed a rather attractive shiner (brown on its edges, blue-grey at its centre), and lucky for me the whole family gets to witness it in all its *cinematic* luminosity because today we just so happen to be picnicking on the tennis court, upon a blanket, with the searing midday sun blazing obligingly down and generously picking out each and every vicious Technicolor detail from this showy-looking but insignificant small-scale ocular injury.

After a painful five minutes on the concrete I dash inside again and fetch myself a cushion; this small foam square is found *exceedingly* welcome in my nether regions (ah, some brief respite at long last for my too-too-tender undercarriage).

La Roux and I are still barely speaking. Hitherto nobody (but *nobody)* has dared to mention our dramatic *pot-pourri* of physical maladies (excepting Feely who, at one point, looks from me to the South African and then back again – the kid puts two and two together so effortlessly that I *must* be teaching him *something* properly – his eyes as round as picnic plates, and delightedly whispers, '*Wow!* Big's really going to *kill* you this time, sister.')

Kill *me*? *This* time?! I give La Roux another furtive once over. In the harsh light, and without his balaclava, his hair looks dramatically moth-infested (Patch certainly did a dandy job there). Ringworm? Now it's finally settling down again it's starting to look as if someone spiteful's been yanking out handfuls of it.

He has a graze on his cheek (with an oddly well-delineated bite mark at its centre), a second on his knuckle, and – worst of all – he appears to have chipped his main front tooth rather badly: just a small pointed spike remains where once there was a tombstone (To tell the absolute truth, I had no *idea* I'd succeeded in wounding him so categorically. Perhaps I'm really much more of a bruiser than I've ever previously given myself credit for?).

And *my* battle-scars? Well there's my extensively bruised bottom (and that's hardly up for inspection), a tetchy shoulder injury, and my swollen lip, which has quietened down considerably (in the swelling department) over the past six hours.

Naturally both La Roux and I have studiously avoided countenancing Big since returning home from our bumpy voyage, but as luck would have it, the Little Man has lain deliciously a-slumbering in his cot 'til noon.

And (doubly lucky), as he bouncily approaches us across the hard green concrete court, he seems to physically *exude* the healthy benefits of his lengthy span of pillow-punching. You might even say his lunch-time disposition is decidedly *jaunty*.

He turns up humming, a melon under his arm, sits down, grabs a knife, smiles at everybody (his expression full of a strangely airy and open geniality), then proceeds to hack up the honeydew and proffer it in chunks to the assembled masses. He says nothing – not *anything* – even when Feely thanks him for his dripping segment in ill-formed burp-language.

Unfortunately, La Roux has recently developed an odd new *tick* to compliment his other, more visible, multi-coloured ailments. And it's suitably maddening. Each and every time he uses his hands (which is quite a bit when he's eating), he neurotically presses the individual pads of his eight fingers down – in order – on to his two thumbs as if testing them for something. He's been doing it all morning.

On the seventh or eighth occasion he does this during lunch, Patch can apparently stand the suspense no longer. 'La Roux,' she says, 'could I ask you a question?'

La Roux wipes some melon juice from his chin, then immediately does this finger thing again.

'Of course you may.'

'What's that weird thing you keep doing with your fingers there?'

The entire assembled company turns, as one, to look at him. 'My tips are numb,' he explains (free air whistling through the gap in his tooth as he's speaking).

'Oh. Okay.' Patch seems perfectly satisfied with this answer, but unfortunately not everyone in the party is as easily fobbed-off as she. Big in particular.

At long last, on the back of this deeply inconclusive sally from my nosey sister, he is finally spurred into his own casual enquiry. 'How did that happen, then?' he asks gently.

'Uh . . . You know what?' La Roux thinks hard for a minute. 'I *don't* honestly remember.'

'Hmmmn. *Concussion*,' Big mutters ruminatively, grabbing some curry balls and a handful of green salad, then reaching out his hand, a second time, to proffer La Roux a slice of cucumber. 'For your shiner,' he says. Then he turns to me.

'Been scrapping again, Medve?' he asks softly.

I gape, then artfully double-bluff him. '*Again*? What on *earth* are you implying?'

Patch chuckles fondly. 'How well I remember', she callously intervenes, 'when you got thrown off the under-twelves' hockey team in Madagascar for breaking the referee's wrist after a bad decision. *God*, that was funny. And then when you bloodied that girl's nose in New Zealand for stealing my rubber chicken . . .'

Big thinks for a while (chewing peaceably). 'To get back to the point,' he continues. 'The rather serious calibre of injuries sustained here would seem to imply *either* . . .' he emphasizes cheerily, '. . . scrapping of a fairly *serious* nature, *or*,' he smiles sweetly, 'a minor traffic accident. But,' he sighs, 'there's no indigenous traffic on this island. And the tide's been in for much of the morning, so . . .' He pauses tantalizingly (I say nothing; I'm simply wondering what's made him so infuriatingly self-satisfied all of a sudden). 'In summing up,' he finishes with a facetious flourish, 'I guess it *must've* been a car accident, then?'

'You know what?' (Uh-oh. I spy a light-bulb suddenly lighting inside La Roux's dark head) '. . . We were actually riding *pillion* on Black Jack's delivery bike, when Medve took a really ill-judged corner and we both fell off it.'

La Roux smiles his deep satisfaction at this ridiculous-sounding porky-pie and then does that crazy-making thing with his fingers again.

'La Roux,' I speak calmly, 'would you mind just not *doing* that?' (It suddenly dawns on me that the whole stupid finger thing is an indirect reference to my most intimate of Girl Places. Don't you *remember*? His fingers *always* go numb after bouts of vaginal interference.)

'Why?' he asks smugly.

'Because it's *irritating* me.'

'I actually quite *like* it,' Feely contributes (in burp, so it's hard to decipher) and starts doing it himself like he thinks he's being clever. Then Patch does the same, but with her left hand only.

Big ignores this (the man's a terrier). 'A *bike* accident?' he repeats casually. La Roux nods. Big frowns. 'You mean that sharp corner on the road down near where Jack parks the Sea Tractor?'

I immediately start cringing, but La Roux totally ignores my agonized expression and continues nodding along gamely. 'Yup. That's the one.'

Big claps his hands delightedly. 'But there *is* no corner. And Jack doesn't *own* a bike. His last one rusted to pieces shortly after we first arrived here.'

La Roux's face stiffens. 'Oh,' he says, and does his finger-twitching thing again, but much faster this time. Big frowns sympathetically. 'Is it a circulation problem you have there?' he asks. 'Are your finger pads prickling?'

La Roux licks his lips nervously. 'Yes. Something like that.'

'And when did this start happening? Was it before or *after* the invisible bicycle accident on the imaginary corner?'

'Uh . . .' La Roux glances my way anxiously and then does the finger thing again.

'*Stop doing that!*' I bellow. Big (still wincing from the sheer volume of my intervention) turns and raises a warning brow at me.

(Enough is enough. This tiny man's eyebrows have long rendered him the south coast's answer to Mr Roger Moore. And the sharply cocked brow – as you may well have gleaned – invariably anticipates imminent *slaughter*.)

'Okay, *okay*,' I come clean immediately (but with a suitable portion of pitiable *mewing*), 'we went fishing and La Roux kept on *whistling*, so I threatened to hit him. But he wouldn't stop – in fact he began singing instead, and really horribly – so I *did* hit him. Then he *still* kept on at it so I was faced with no real alternative but to sit on his head to try and quieten him.

'Which was when his fingers went numb. From feverishly scrabbling on the bottom of the boat. Either that or from the shock, I imagine. And that's the whole story.'

La Roux's hyperactive hands seem suddenly frozen. Big is quiet for a long while as if mulling the whole thing over. Feely was right. I *am* in for it this time (the child's a four-year-old fucking seer).

After a while, having said nothing, Big slowly begins eating again. Gradually Patch and Feely follow suit (La Roux and I merely chew on our tongues and glare at each other). Big feeds well and at his leisure, then – when he's finally replete, has wiped his lips clean with a paper napkin, has pushed his plate away and cordially complimented the chefette on her sterling endeavours – he turns, scratches his stomach idly and fixes his most sternly penetrating gaze on me.

'*Whistling*, you say?' he asks softly.

I clear my throat. 'Yes. And singing too.'

Big rubs his chin, slowly. 'It's difficult to condone violence, Medve,' he tells me calmly, 'under *any* circumstances, but to sit on someone's *face* because they disturb you when you're fishing . . .' He shakes his head as if in utter disbelief at the things he's been hearing. 'Only a *saint* could have reacted less savagely under those conditions.'

La Roux's smug expression melts like a cheap chocolate (from almost-cocky to very-tragic) in a mere matter of seconds. My own face starts glowing with an incendiary piety.

'La Roux,' Big turns to him decisively, 'there are obviously some rather important things you need to understand about my middle daughter. The most important of these is that everything she ever learned in the fishing department she learned from me, her father.

'I'm afraid we all take the art of angling very seriously around here,' he smiles angelically. 'Now finish up your lunch and let's go inside for a while. I've actually got something quite *wonderful* in mind for those troublesome fingers of yours.'

La Roux's thin lips tighten fractionally. 'Oh yes?' he manages. 'And what might that be exactly?' (I think he's having awful visions of thumb-screws or something.)

'I am going to teach you how to *crochet*,' Big beams. 'It's always been a great solution to the tricky problem of bad circulation.'

He stands up. 'Come on,' he beckons benevolently, 'follow me.'

*

So I got off lightly. The important thing is I *know* I did, and this apprehension will help to guide all my future decisions and thoughts and behaviour, and will ultimately shape me into a better person. (*Yeah.* If you actually *believe* this kind of fatuous Dr Spock bullshit you're in for a rather rude awakening. The truth is my teen-trouble-making facility is now as well-honed and destructively arbitrary as a badly wired Exocet thing-ummy. But when I finally blow – and *boy*, will I blow – take succour from the fact that I'm fully intending to take that bastard Spock right down with me. Screaming and burning.)

Okay, so I'm still pretty-much the self-same *rankly remorseless bitch* I ever was after my trying lunch-time excitations, but even so I celebrate my unexpected getting-off-lightly by self-lessly helping my hard-working (if relentlessly fleshy) sibling with the washing-up.

As I'm sure you can imagine, this is about as rare a sight in these parts as a dodo getting accidentally caught up inside the flight propeller of a mid-air 747.

While I clumsily swill my two huge hands around inside a sink of hot water, Patch dries gamely, and we indulge in a rather mystifying conversation about my long, dark night spent in the questionable company of Mr Jack Henry (Patch is totally into dream interpretation. She's like a pre-pubescent Freud but without the beard and the sexual fixation).

'So you dreamed Jack Henry was imprisoned again, but this time he was locked up inside your brain?' she summarizes.

'That's about the gist of it. And I kept telling him he was free and that he should bugger off, but he wouldn't listen.'

Patch pauses and considers. 'I really like it,' she says, 'it's kind of clever.'

136

'Well I appreciate your dream approval, Patch,' I snipe, 'but what about the hidden *meaning*?'

'It's something philosophical,' she smiles, 'which I guess must mean that your considerable intelligence – so absent in your day-to-day thoughts and actions – gets all its exercise unconsciously.'

'Is that a *joke*?' I ask uneasily.

'Uh, no, but here's my interpretation anyway,' she quickly continues. 'For some reason you seem to be preoccupied by the notion that a person's freedom isn't defined by their physical conditions . . .'

'*Pardon?*' I turn around to peer at her and accidentally drip suds on to the tiling.

'You're dripping,' she scolds. I guiltily shove my hands over the sink again.

'It's a kind of *cynicism*,' she explains. 'You think Jack Henry – for all of his insight and wise words and everything – is actually in a prison of his own construction, and that even now he's free he won't be able to escape it . . .' She pauses. 'Which in my book is an interesting but fairly depressing analysis. I myself have a much greater faith in the strength and resilience of the human animal.'

'You're right,' I tell her. 'I *am* much cleverer when I'm sleeping.'

She sniggers. '*I'll* say you are.'

For some indefinable reason her reaction strikes me as slightly excessive. I frown. 'Meaning?'

The snigger expands into a chuckle.

'*Meaning?*'

Her eyes widen. 'La *Roux*.'

'What about him?'

She gnaws delightedly on her thumb-nail, her cheeks glowing. 'You really thought you'd done a job on him, didn't you?'

I slowly shake dry my hands as she ducks behind the table.

'A job? How exactly?'

'The black eye, the tooth and the other stuff.'

She's laughing so hard all of a sudden that I can barely understand what she's saying.

'But the thing is . . .' she continues, now almost bent double, 'the thing is . . .'

I put my hands on my hips. 'Tell me the *thing*, why don't you?'

Her convulsing fingers scrabble on the table-top. 'The thing is, it was all *make-up*. Almost all of it!'

'Make-up?'

'His injuries!'

'*Make-up?!*' My jaw drops. 'Are you *serious*?'

She nods in mute hilarity.

'And . . . and the tooth?'

'A cap! He can pull it off whenever the fancy takes him. A final absolute stroke of bloody *genius*, if you ask me.'

But I am not asking. In fact, I am lost for words, temporarily. 'So was Big in on everything?' I eventually manage.

'He *was*!' she explodes, 'and little Feely too. We *all* were.'

Oh. Oh. Oh. *Oh*. My feet are suddenly glued to the kitchen tiles, my fists are slowly clenching and unclenching, I am gasping and choking and blinking and *panting*. My rage is wild and absolute and all-consuming.

*Trumped!* My whole family employed in a plot to humiliate me by that persistently whistling, masturbating, fountain-pissing, sleep-walking, high-thigh-squeezing interloper? How *could* they! Even Big? Even *he*? (I mean, suddenly developing a sense of humour without even *warning* me?)

Patch is still laughing a full five minutes later, clutching ineffectually at her big belly, her round face gargoyled with uncontrollable hysteria.

'Okay,' I eventually splutter, when I am finally capable of speaking coherently again, 'what – if you can actually remember – is that irritating thing people always say about revenge?'

She stops laughing. 'Oooh. Best served *cold*,' she tells me, her small nose twitching.

'Right,' I smile, 'and that, my dear sister, is exactly how it's going to be. I have a plan. It's a nasty one. And I will be needing your assistance . . .'

Patch immediately starts rubbing her two fat hands together, her laughter forgotten, her cheeks drawn in *hungrily*. A second serving? Another helping? A double *whammy*? I mean, what could be *better*?

Absolutely nothing.

## 14

So I don't want to keep harping *on* about it, but do you know what *really* gets to me about this whole, damn, phoney, black-eyed, broken-toothed La Roux-inspired travesty? It's the way it was all arranged with so much guile and finesse and – I hate to say it – real, honest-to-goodness *subtlety* (perhaps there's actually more than meets the average untrained eye to this rank outsider's military history).

I mean, making me *think* I'd had such a sweet little victory when Big so unexpectedly took my side over the face-sitting incident. And that ludicrous 'teaching him to crochet' business. And the infuriating finger pinching. And my – come on, I *have* to admit it – ridiculous smugness when I thought I'd inadvertently done him a serious injury (all that 'Am I more of a bruiser than I thought I was?' crap. How *embarrassing*).

To think I actually imagined I'd got off scot-free. And all those silly pangs of *guilt* I nearly considered suffering (no matter how briefly) at *his expense*. All that wasted moral energy!

My *God*, what a triumph. And how to top it? There's little doubt in my fevered mind that it'll take some doing. But never, *ever* let it be said that canny Miss Medve can't rise to a challenge. He's thrown down the gauntlet, and blow me backwards if I'm not calmly bending over and casually retrieving it.

What *is* a gauntlet anyway? (I only hope it's hygienic.)

*

Right. So here's how I arrange things: first off, Patch is sworn to secrecy over having let slip the fact that La Roux is not really as seriously injured as he seems to be. More importantly, she is immediately sent along to tell him how much I would appear to regret my misdoings, how tender and tearful I currently seem, *consumed* as I am by my powerful and overwhelming feelings of awful remorsefulness.

Big is to be kept in line by being told by this most devious sister of mine that my sudden rash of guilty feelings are teaching me exactly the kind of fruitful lesson in personal responsibility *any* parent should be proud of instilling (the kind of lesson I have so far, apparently – according to Patch, and Big actively agrees with her – been basically *incapable* of learning).

So where's the harm – she asks – in temporarily *extending* my useful bout of moral education? Where indeed, the shortarsed traitor tells her, *damn* him.

Patch soon scurries back to base (my table-tennis headquarters), her clutch of missions successfully undertaken, absolutely *glowing* with self-satisfaction. And when Mr La Roux happens to pass this way himself, just a few minutes later (patently intent on pressing home his advantage), this very useful and utterly duplicitous little fattie scarpers, a fiftypence piece clutched inside her hot hand and some careful instructions to head for the mainland (a ten-minute walk while the tide is low) to buy me something very *particular* from the tourist-trap newsagents in Bigbury-on-Sea to further facilitate my dastardly machinations.

When Patch has gone I can finally give La Roux my full attention (I'm actually rather busy painting my pottery, but I glance up regularly whenever the need arises. Come on. I don't want to be too obvious, now, do I?).

'So how was the crochet lesson, then?' I ask him solicitously.

La Roux pulls something out of his pocket. 'Big gave me this,' he holds up a needle.

'Ah. The crochet implement.'

'And this too.'

From the other pocket he withdraws some wool. Yellow.

'Ah. The means of production.'

'He says I have a natural talent. He thinks I should get into lace-making. He's always wanted to do it himself but he says he doesn't have the patience.'

I smile weakly at this notion and continue my painting. La Roux casts on, meanwhile, performs a couple of clumsy stitches (for show, principally) then quickly shoves his pitiful endeavours back into his pockets.

'Need a hand with that?' he eventually whistles. (The de-capped tooth is still interfering a little with his vocalizing.)

I look up. 'What? With *those* fingers? Aren't they still troubling you like they were earlier?'

'Uh . . .' he quickly glances down at them.

I lay my brush on the table.

'La Roux . . .'

He looks up again.

'Yes?'

'It's just . . . I was . . . I was only wondering . . .' I peer modestly towards the ceiling.

'What?'

'Well, whether there was any way . . .' I falter. His face stares intently back at me, his every feature cut into an almost marble-carved rictus of anticipation (The harder I look, incidentally, the more clearly I see what a botched-up job that make-over was. Jesus *wept*! And to think I still went right on and *fell* for it!)

'What are you trying to say, exactly?' he mutters.

I take a deep breath (this is killing me). 'What I'm trying to tell you is that I'm really, *really* sorry. I suppose I must've got pretty carried away, earlier. But I so much regret the broken tooth and the eye injury that I'd be willing to do just about *anything . . .'*

'And the knuckle,' he interrupts.

'That too,' I gurgle.

'And the bite on my cheek.'

'*Naturally*,' I squeak.

He pauses and his eyes tighten, 'And the *fingers . . .'*

'Yes.' I chew my lip (quite adorably, under the circumstances – well it's either that or I'm going to have to spit on him). 'It's just I had no idea my sitting on you like that would have so many unexpected . . . um . . . . *repercussions.'*

(Ah. Like launching a *fart*. Just one little shove and he's *flying*.)

'But don't you remember', he whines artfully, 'how I explained the other day about my father and that awful gynaecological business?'

'Of course I do,' I purr. 'Christmas Day. You and your brother. Spookie the dog. The rotting and festering. I remember perfectly.'

'Spookie?' he sounds confused. 'I don't ever recall mentioning *him*.'

'Oh,' my eyes widen, 'perhaps I got the wrong end of the stick there, for some reason.'

La Roux ponders awhile.

143

'You know, I'm uncertain whether I might've mentioned previously how I went to see a doctor over the problem with my fingers and he said that the thing to do . . .' he catches my eye and then suddenly stops talking, but his unspoken and (plainly) malign intent hangs in the air like a bad-meat kite in a high wind. Stinking *hideously*.

My eyes widen (Lord, this is easy). 'What *thing* exactly?'

'Something specialists in the area call . . . um . . .' (I can see even *he* thinks this is cheeky. So I try and help him out.)

'Aversion therapy?'

He smiles (just a touch of unease there, around the edges of his mouth). 'Uh . . . no. The direct opposite. More like a sort of . . . well, a sort of curing with *kindness.*'

His tone, at this point – as I'm sure you can imagine – is quite revoltingly ingratiating.

'I don't know anything about that,' I tell him (feeling the need to take the initiative a little, not to give in *too* easily, to wriggle, to struggle), 'but I once read something *fascinating* about aversion therapy,' I lie, 'in some of Thurber's dog writings . . .'

La Roux scowls. 'Thurber? Who's he?'

I don't bother answering (I mean, the *ignorance* of the man), I simply say, 'In one of Thurber's stories there was a badly trained bloodhound called Charlatan . . .'

La Roux frowns. 'That's an odd name for an animal.'

'Well he was a very odd man. He was born in Ohio.'

'Right.' La Roux crosses his arms (not good body language, so I babble on, rapidly).

'Anyway, Charlatan had this awful habit of stealing the remains of the pork roast every Sunday when Thurber was cooling it in the pantry after dinner. For sandwiches, later.'

'Here's a question,' La Roux interrupts. 'How on earth did Charlatan get into the pantry in the first place?'

'He opened the door with his paws. It was a knack he'd perfected. He was a very intelligent creature, but *horribly* devious.'

'Hmmmn,' La Roux ponders, 'they needed to fix up some kind of bolt arrangement. That would almost certainly have stopped his antics.'

'Ah,' I shake my head, 'but that's where you're missing the point entirely. Thurber felt resorting to a bolt would've undermined general man–dog household relations. All trust would've been lost. What they needed was a situation of *greater* not lesser understanding.'

'Oh,' La Roux starts frowning again.

'Anyhow, Thurber decided to solve his problem by trying a little aversion therapy on Charlatan. And for the next three weeks, every time he put the pork roast into the pantry he would do something unexpected to the carcass – like a mouse trap inside it, or a small incendiary device. Or applying rat poison. Or some of that powder you get in joke shops that makes you guff like a monkey . . .'

La Roux looks appalled. Perhaps I've waxed too lyrical. My imagination is plainly *rampant* today.

'The point is, in the end Charlatan learned his lesson and he never stole the pork roast again.'

La Roux is still not happy. 'I'd've fixed a bolt and to *hell* with all the other business,' he opines stubbornly.

I nod. 'I know what you mean. Perhaps Thurber's techniques *were* a little excessive, but his intentions, in principal, were pure and loving. He adored that dog. He simply wanted a positive renewal of *trust* between them.'

'But how does all this affect me?' La Roux asks (seeming rather to have lost the plot again).

'I have a plan,' I tell him, firmly girding my loins (not an attractive notion, I'll admit, with all that residual bruising). 'It's still in its early stages. It's *madly* formative, and you may well think it's stupid. But I personally think it's a *corker* . . .'

Already he looks interested.

'To try and pay you back for all the awful damage I inflicted this morning – although, frankly, the whistling *was* unbearably provoking – I want to do something helpful, in my own small way, to try and renew your faith in the female anatomy.'

La Roux's eyebrows rise hilariously. I pause for a moment. I need to be careful and stealthy. This man is a professional bullshitter himself. I might've got him hooked, but I don't want to risk losing him by reeling him in too quickly.

'I mean, I could draw you a few pictures to start off with and *explain* some things to you that might seem frightening or confusing. And then you could sneak a tiny little peek at me – I mean while I'm still in my underwear, and from several feet away – just to get into the swing of things. And we could take it one step at a time until . . .'

'Until?' (The man's virtually salivating.)

'Well, I had some silly idea about maybe going down to the Mermaid Cove – where those strange fishes hang out that wriggle against your shins – the kind of environment you might feel at ease in, and then perhaps I could . . .' I frown. 'Now what is it that they do with new statues at formal public openings? For some reason the word temporarily escapes me . . .'

'Disrobing?' he gabbles.

'No.'

'Unsheathing?'

'No.'

La Roux's bad-skinned visage breaks into a grin. 'I don't *care* what the word is,' he crows, 'it's a fucking *marvellous* idea.'

*Easy*. See? One. Two. Three. And I've *sunk* him.

## 15

Nobody ever pretended Operation Vagina (that's currently what I'm calling it) would be an *easy* action. And Lord knows it isn't. But surely – I tell a slightly bemused Feely as he helps me with some crucial military drawings – even *fools* appreciate that trapping a wild and wily animal while it's still alive and *kicking* always takes infinitely greater time and patience than going out with a firearm and simply shooting it to pieces (Even if, as in La Roux's case, the use of random fire-power might prove – pound for pound – significantly more *gratifying*, I'm afraid guns aren't really a serious option. Why? Because I'm *sixteen years young*, God-dammit, and unable to get a fucking *licence*).

I don't know *who* I'm trying to convince exactly, him or me.

'Whatever you say, Medve,' Feely belches indulgently. 'I agree completely . . .', then he grabs a red crayon and applies it with focused gusto to my pen-and-ink efforts (Yes, the child's an absolute *buttress* and still burping, bless him).

If, by any chance, you happen to be interested in my canny Operation's essential timing, well, all in all, and everything considered, the full and frenzied *climax* to my major manipulative masterwork takes one dark night and two long days to come into its mature and mellow fruition.

The initial pace is deceptively slow and leisurely, but this does nothing to diminish the unhealthy *satisfaction* gleaned from each and every well-timed step in my foul and wicked perambulation. The loose scenario runs as follows:

1. *The Whitewash*
(I believe we've been here already.) With a feisty mixture of guano and lies, Sister Patch gets La Roux and the others to think I'm deeply ignorant and guilt-ridden.

2. *The Baiting*
(Ditto) I masterfully – if I say so myself – convince La Roux that I'm willing to sacrifice my girlie privacy to improve his mental, emotional and sexual well-being.

3. *The Drawing*
*Oooh.* Now that's more like it . . .

The self-same evening of the fishing trip, I welcome La Roux into the ping-pong room and show him a series of badly penned sketches (This is 1981, remember, and pre-Milan Kundera's shameless sexual shenanigans with mirrors, so everything's looking pretty damn perfunctory down there, even to begin with, and – to make matters worse – I never really paid much attention during school biology lessons, on the brief occasions I ever *had* them).

La Roux pulls out a chair and sits down next to me. I notice idly that he has greased back his hair and is wearing his favourite pony jumper. Ah. How *touching*.

I have borrowed one of Barge's old artist's sketch pads for my amateurish doodlings.

'Okay, La Roux,' I say calmly, placing the sketch pad before him. 'I'm going to show you some intimate pictures, and if at any point you sense yourself becoming agitated or unhappy, or if you feel your finger-pads tingling, just tell me about it and I'll stop what I'm doing and we can play a game of ping-pong or darts or arm wrestle or something, to try and keep the mood as unthreatening and tranquil as possible.'

La Roux takes a deep breath and grabs a hold of my hand. He squeezes it gently. 'Right,' he says, nodding twice. 'I think I'm about as ready as I'll ever be.'

(Obviously it's difficult for me to turn the pages or to point at my diagrams effectively now that La Roux has taken my spare paw prisoner. But so be it.)

Page one. The Female Torso, in all its glorious totality (I have traced around the outline of one of Patch's old Sindy dolls for this full-body illustration, but I've given the lady in question a pair of nipples, a friendly smile and a well-defined pubic area).

La Roux stares at the drawing with an air of great satisfaction (nothing to worry about here, presumably).

'So,' I smile brightly, 'I think this is all fairly self-explanatory . . . Uh . . .' I do some pointing. 'Head, thorax, abdomen. Just the same, I think you'll find, as with insects and horses. But slightly different from fishes. Right . . .'

I'm about to turn over when La Roux says, 'Here's a question for you . . .'

'What?' I ask anxiously.

'I've long wondered', he ruminates, 'whether women pee through their vaginas. It's just that's one of the things I've always found slightly off-putting about them, sexually.'

He casually twitches his fingers as he stares at me. I take a deep breath, clamp my jaw together and then shake my head.

'Don't be ridiculous,' I grind (that terrible mixture of enraged and giggly). 'Of *course* women don't pee through their sexual organs. That would be *disgusting*. They urinate through an extra hole just below their bottoms. I'll show you exactly where, later, in the more detailed illustration, if you'll bear with me.'

I turn over.

Page Two. The Genital Region.

La Roux clenches my hand a little tighter.

'I feel nauseous,' he confides, blinking repeatedly.

*Fine*. We play two games of ping-pong and I cheerfully wipe the floor with him (21–6, 21–4). Then we sit down again. Slightly out of breath and perspiring gently.

La Roux slowly sets about inspecting the illustration properly. He starts at the top end and then works his way downwards, frowning. 'Two things,' he mutters, after a while.

'Fire away.'

'First off, for a woman who paints china for a living you seem to have no real, *discernible* artistic ability. This female genital looks like an angry moose, yawning. Secondly, there's far more activity here than I ever remember learning about in biology. There are so many cavities it's like a shower-head . . .' he points. 'I mean, what's *that*, to start off with?'

I look closer. 'That's . . .' I turn the drawing up the other way. 'I think that's a nipple. No. No. It's a belly button, *stupid*.'

La Roux stares harder. 'And below it?'

'Clitoris. The girl penis.'

His eyes widen. 'You're kidding me?'

'Nope.'

'The *girl penis*,' La Roux repeats, softly, committing it to memory.

He stares some more. 'And there?'

'Oh . . . no . . .' I chuckle, 'that's something Feely put in when I wasn't looking. I think it's supposed to be a revolutionary standard. Like a flag. Simply try and ignore it.'

La Roux's brow wrinkles. 'It's just the particular *colour* he's chosen is giving me a bad feeling . . . You know . . . Red. *Infection.*'

I quickly put my hand over it.

'Just think a little harder about the cervix instead,' I tell him brightly (incidentally, not featured in this diagram – internal bits and pieces are better illustrated on page three).

La Roux points again. 'The moose's jowls,' he mutters, 'is *that* the thing you just mentioned?'

I snigger. 'Nope. Labia. A fleshy area.'

'And *this*? Urgh!'

He inhales sharply and his face almost quivers with horror.

'Oh dear,' I ho-hum, 'it's just some low-fat fruit yoghurt. A piece of peach I must've accidentally spat out while I was drawing. Sorry.'

I pull the offending item off with my nail, and then blow it away. 'There. Gone.'

La Roux pushes his chair back. 'I think,' he mutters, 'I've seen enough to be going on with. Perhaps you should put them away again. For the time being, anyway . . .'

'But I haven't even shown you the special urinary *duct* yet,' I protest indignantly.

La Roux stands. 'Come *on*,' he taunts, grabbing a bat and waving it. 'I suddenly feel like the time has come for The Great La Roux to thrash you *senseless* at ping-pong.'

I put away the pictures, without any further objections. Then I grab my bat, we play the game and I beat him, three times over in quick succession. 21–1, 21–4, 21–3. Which in my book is pretty bloody categorically.

4. *My Disgusting Crochet Knickers*
(Now we're *really* getting somewhere.)

It's a good while later (after eight, approximately) and following an extended bout of early evening snacking. (The menu? Rice cakes, walnuts in vinegar, dried pears and tinned figs in their natural juices.) Big trots casually outside on to the balcony to savour the large, pink sun a-setting over the sea with that bastard brown-nose La Roux close in tow. More crochet fun is plainly in the offing.

After doing a couple of circuits (for some inexplicable reason, La Roux has a tiny, white, clay pipe with him – the kind they unearth in tedious archaeological excavations – and while he walks he chews on it like a vacuous South African amalgam of Sherlock Holmes and Popeye), they sit down together, either side of a wicker table, with three rolls of wool, a book Big's reading about the Hay Diet, and a flickering oil lamp burning between them.

Big is completing Nebraska (pale mauve) while La Roux is receiving cursory instructions on how to make a clumsy, circular doily. It's all horribly intense and muscular and arts and craftsy, as I'm sure you can imagine.

I'm serving tea, as it happens. Rosehip. I bring it out on a tray. I shove the balls of wool aside, to make room for it (they both cluck like old women, in tandem, then continue what they're doing, *without* even thanking me).

I turn to go. I walk five steps away, then pause, and spin, and face them again. Although Big – from where I'm now

153

carefully stationed – has his back to me, La Roux, on the other hand, has a perfect view of my fine girl-giant figure over his compadre's tiny needle-working shoulder.

I place my knees together, lift my skirt, adjust my knickers, and wait patiently for La Roux's attention. A full four minutes pass (it seems that initially he's much too deeply embroiled in the wonders of crochet to notice my silent attendance), then Big reaches out his hand for a sip of his tea.

He takes a mouthful, pulls a face, puts his cup down, tips in a little honey, stirs, offers a kindly word of wisdom to La Roux. ('I think if you hold the needle less tightly the stitches will loosen up accordingly. It's all just a question of *flow*, I find, with crochet.' *Jeepers*. And people think Chairman *Mao* was fussy?)

La Roux glances up at him, nods, looks down again. Chews on his pipe some. Freezes. His hands become slightly clumsy. He takes a deep breath, and then, finally, shoulders up and blinking, he peeks my way again.

My way? I've *gone*. I've vamoosed. I've scarpered. Fast as a rat, I've scuttled inside and have hidden, sniggering, behind the curtains.

La Roux scowls, disconcertedly. Did he really just imagine a scary six-foot girl giant, her teeth full of fig pips, grinning savagely in the dark and scary shadows of the oil-lamp's flickering? Did he? The very *devil* in a voluminous pair of badly soiled, baggy, crochet knickers. Standing, larger than life, only five short steps behind her temperamental, tea-sipping father (a short-fused bugger at the best of times)? Did he?

Big glances up again and notices La Roux's eyes wandering around anxiously in the shadows behind him. 'La Roux, what are you *thinking*?' he suddenly stutters. 'You've dropped a stitch there, can't you see?' He gets up, shows him how to rectify the problem, returns to his chair and sits down again. 'And don't forget to drink up your tea,' he reminds him, several minutes later, in a most sweet and cordial and gentlemanly manner.


5. *La Roux gets The Collywobbles*

You know how it is with a military operation. It can't run too smoothly. There have to be undercurrents, back-washes and eddies. To keep things uneasy.

Before bed La Roux corners me in the kitchen and whispers, 'I think I've suddenly lost interest in this whole genital situation.'

I gasp and look suitably devastated. 'La Roux. *No*. You've *got* to be kidding. I mean, after all the *effort* I've put into it?'

He shrugs. 'It's just too damn risky.'

I frown. 'Sorry? *Risky*? What do you mean?'

He grimaces. 'You *know*. The little dumb-scene, earlier, behind Big, at tea.'

I continue frowning. 'I have absolutely no idea what you're talking about.'

He sighs impatiently. 'The figgy teeth. The huge crochet panties.'

'*Panties?*' I echo. '*Huge?* Don't be ridiculous. *Figgy teeth?* I never eat figs. Ask anybody. Ask Patch.'

Patch trundles conveniently into view at exactly this moment, Feely in tow.

'Patch,' La Roux enquires, just as I've suggested, 'does Medve here eat figs ever?'

Patch looks at La Roux as if she thinks he's crazy. 'Figs?

*Never*. They give her eczema. She's horribly, horribly, *horribly* allergic.'

I give her a warning glance (talk about a fat and shifty Sarah Bernhardt in the making), then yank La Roux into the laundry room, slam the door behind him, and lift up my skirt most *gingerly*, modestly showing him only the most *inoffensive* corner of my freshly changed undergarments.

Cheesecloth. Petite. With birds and roses. The kind of things you could blow your nose on and then throw away. Flimsy as a weak alibi.

'Oh,' La Roux frowns, then looks a little closer, 'that's a nasty bruise you've got there, on your thigh . . .'

'Well, next time you happen to feel like taking a peek at it,' I tell him, haughtily dropping my hem and flouncing doorwards, 'you'd better ask me *very* nicely, you rude and ungrateful South African *sissy*.'

As I march resolutely through the kitchen – chin up, hips twitching – fat Patch, still lounging against the work surfaces, stands straight, salutes, and then winks at me lewdly, like a too-eager busboy after a big tip.

# 16

*'It's always in that brief and blissful moment when you feel you're at your most unassailable that you actually have the worst to fear . . .'*

I was taught this motto in Malay Brownies, and it so often proved invaluable to me throughout the seventies – all those tricky pyjama parties and risky pre-teen-girl-tiffs: 'You're my best friend!', 'No I'm not! She is! And you're ugly!' – that you'd honestly think, at this apposite juncture, it would be absolutely *foremost* in my mental processes.

But it isn't (Perhaps I've got above myself, temporarily. Truth to tell, I'm seriously considering borrowing the life story of Che Guevara from the local library to give me a taste of something really *meaty* in terms of conflict philosophy. You *know*, to try and get familiar with some of the more *filthy* aspects of war-making, the likes of which Baden Powell never *dreamed* of even in his most frenzied, strong-brown-booted pseudo-authoritarian fantasies).

Don't call me overconfident. Just call me *silly*.

Two a.m. One moment I am deep asleep (dreaming about a true-life incident in which Jack Henry is found guilty by a Kansas-based Grand Jury, and sentenced to ten bonus years in prison for carrying a dangerous weapon concealed about his battered person. A Bic biro, but without its inky middle.

Jack Henry is *incandescent* with rage. He can't honestly believe they'd send him down for this trifle. A Bic pen? Are you *kidding*?

But although I keep asking him *why* he was carrying the pen and what exact *purpose* it was serving – it's a long night and I have nothing better to do with myself – he just keeps cursing at me and saying it's *irrelevant* or that I'm *bothering* him unnecessarily. He wants some *peace*. Can't I *see* that? Am I *stupid* or something?

'But this is *my* head, you rascal,' I bleat at him. '*So?!*' he yells back at me. 'You think I actually *want* to be in this hell-hole? Do you imagine I *like* being trapped inside the teenage skull of a girl who's never even bothered reading Marx or Jung or Sartre or Dostoevsky . . .?') Then – *bam!* – the very next instant I am wide awake and giggling. Yes. I said *giggling*. Uncontrollably.

Because I am receiving a relentless tickling at the hands of a Master Tickler. Guess who? No. On second thoughts, don't bother. It *can* be none other than the Pesky South African.

I don't know if the actual tickling is entirely intentional (I've just woken up, how sodding *rational* do you expect me to be?), but he's applying something soft as thistle-down to the base of my spine; that tantalizing junction where my baby-doll nightie is *just* supposed to cover its matching puffball panties (I get two baby-dolls every year from my Great Aunt Sonya who thinks because I'm so huge she's literally *obliged* to buy me everything in miniature).

I slap at the place at least five times before I realize it's not in fact a deeply misguided leaden-arsed mosquito or a mischievously fluffy-footed fairy tap-dancing cheerily at the top end of my buttocks. It's something altogether different. It's a peacock feather.

I sit up and blink. La Roux stands before me (in his regulation army pyjamas), waving the feather around like an air-traffic controller. I rub my eyes. 'Are you sleep-walking again?' I whisper querulously.

'*What?*'

(Plainly *not* by the strength of his reaction.) He sits down, cross-legged, on the end of my mattress and pulls a spare blanket around his bony shoulders.

'So, what are you doing?' he asks.

I blink, indignantly. 'What am I *doing*? I was fucking *sleeping*.'

'Oh.' He sighs, yawns, scratches his head a little and stares up at the colourful dome above him. 'There's a piece of glass, a green piece, directly above us. The wind's really rattling it. Can you see it shifting?'

I look to where he's pointing. 'It's always done that. It's just part of the stained-glass deal. Lovely but noisy. Like an intelligent female.'

'All the same, I think we should move over a little . . .'

Before I can muster the strength to oppose him, he's thrown off his blanket, is clambering around on his hands and knees like an poisonous but insipid four-legged spider, and is shoving my mattress (with me still upon it – and that's no mean achievement) several feet over towards the bar.

I'm too whacked to complain. I just glare at him silently as he clambers back on board and readjusts his blanket.

'That's much, much better,' he mutters, and then yawns again.

'What's *wrong* with you, La Roux?'

He shrugs. 'Can't sleep. I was wondering whether you might like to read me a story. To calm my nerves down. To cheer me up.'

159

I rub my eyes. 'What kind of story did you have in mind?'

'Anything.' He smiles. 'And I bought you my special pea-cock feather. It's a present. I got it from the back-end of a bad-tempered bird in Wolverhampton.'

He hands it over. I take it. It's a fine one.

'Wolverhampton? What on earth were you doing there?'

'Nothing in particular. That's just where I was staying before I came here.'

'Oh.' I sniff the feather. It smells of nothing. 'Thank you. Although they're bad luck. Did you know that?'

'No.' He yanks at the blanket and sniffs, mournfully. 'The nights are the worst,' he finally confides, after a pause.

'In what respect?'

'I miss my family. And other stuff . . . like . . .' his voice soft-ens, 'like the way the farmers burn the veld in winter. The smell of charcoal and the sight of the dry grass flaming. The fire engines. And the noise the flocks of mousebirds make. A special whistle. Like a *tree-ree-ree*.'

I try and shush him, but he doesn't listen.

'And the stag beetles,' he chuckles, 'big as your fist, caught in potholes on the roads. The red earth. And the coastal drive to Cape Point. And the thieving apes who attack the tourists and steal their sandwiches. And the huge moths. And my best friend, Thiens.'

'*Who?*'

'Thiens. He's a student at Witwatersrand University. Near Johannesburg. If you become a student you can avoid con-scription. He's doing foreign languages.'

'So why didn't you become a student then?'

He tuts at me. 'Too *stupid*, stupid.'

'Thanks a bunch.'

He leans back on his elbows. 'Oh, how I miss the purple jacaranda,' he muses, 'and the sunbirds. And the bee-eaters. Table Mountain. The big winds. The water shortages. The *braai vleis*,' he smiles, 'which I always really *hated* when I was there. And the flowers in the Karoo Desert. And the summer storms. And hail the size of golf balls. And the proteas in the Stellenbosch Botanical Gardens. And the boys selling newspapers on the roadways.'

'The men,' I correct him.

'And these special bubblegums we have called Wicks's. Turns your mouth pink. Tastes of antiseptic. And grape-flavoured Fanta. And Datsuns . . .'

'I bet your mother misses you,' I intervene softly (if I was his mother, I believe I would miss him).

He smiles. 'She thinks I'm a coward. I'm a local embarrassment. Everybody knows about it. And the maid – my nanny – Dorothea. She thinks the same way. For once in their lives they're in total agreement. They're both *equally* ashamed of me.'

'And are you a coward?'

'Probably.'

He stares up at the ceiling. 'The Peacock Lounge,' he says, yawning, 'that's why I brought you the feather. And because you've made me feel at home here. And for showing me your panties. And for never having seen *Joseph*. Which is a tragedy.'

He's quiet for a while and I think he must be sleeping. Then his voice breaks the silence. 'Tell me the story of Shiro Chan,' he whispers, turning over on to his belly. 'I want to hear it again.'

'I don't know where the book is.'

'Then make it up.'

I grumble a little (as may well be expected under the cir-cumstances), then place down the feather and lie on my back, staring up at the blue-green-glass ceiling.

'In the beautiful Japanese city of Nara,' I whisper, softly, 'there once lived around about a thousand wild red deer. In the spring, the bucks would proudly display their antlers while the gentle does would tend to their fawns. One year, however, a special doe was born with a wonderful crown of strange white fur on top of her head. They called her Shiro Chan, Queen of the Deer of Nara.

'The beautiful Shiro Chan was always very popular with the tourists, who loved her, dearly. But after only a few short years of life she was tragically killed in a road traffic accident. It would seem that true beauty . . .' I pause, momentarily.

'It would seem,' La Roux repeats dozily, 'that true beauty . . .'

'It would seem that true beauty is fated to a short life only. Even among the deer.'

'Ah,' he sighs peacefully. 'The beautiful Shiro Chan. Queen of *all* the Bovines.'

In the morning, when I awaken, no sign of him remains. Only the peacock feather, an abandoned blanket near to the door-way, and a strangely all-pervasive smell of antiseptic on the bed linen.

I'm thinking of aborting the plan (The Malay Brownies were spot on, see?). It's just the fun's kind of gone out of it. I'm not sure when it happened, exactly. That's just the way I'm feel-ing. My mind is virtually made up. Then something rather inexplicable happens. And I can't make head or tail of it. But it changes things.

After breakfast (a genial occasion: Big's been out early to pick mussels from the rocks and Patch boils them perfectly and serves them in the foyer, on a blanket, at the feet of Diana. Feely doesn't remove the tricky, green, anal area on one of his and nearly vomits. All *very* stimulating), I'm diligently putting in some extra hours on my pottery when I hear a heated conversation going on way down below me. In the kitchens.

Patch and La Roux, arguing about I don't know *what*, precisely. And Patch is going off at him like a firecracker.

Five minutes later, La Roux wanders past my doorway. I call him in. He looks different, somehow, from before.

'I just heard you arguing with Patch. What happened?'

He shrugs. 'Nothing.'

'I don't know if you realize this, but Patch doesn't argue with *anybody*. She's too placid. That's simply her disposition.'

La Roux is staring over my shoulder and out of the window. 'The weather's fine,' he says, 'maybe we can go swimming later, with the fishes, like you said we should yesterday.'

I nod. He smiles. 'Patch just . . .' he pauses, as if something terrible is weighing on his mind. 'She's just going on about apartheid and all this complicated political stuff I don't understand. She's been reading about the Sharpeville Massacre and she got upset when I didn't know much about it . . .' he grimaces, 'which I suppose is pretty embarrassing, really.'

He shrugs helplessly, then he leaves me.

*Jesus!* What got into *him* all of a sudden?

When I see Patch just before lunch, her face is blotchy like she's been crying all morning. She's about as tetchy as a nesting reed warbler when there's a cuckoo in the area. She won't let me go *near* her. She's cooking a Thai vegetable concoction with ginger and fresh coriander.

I pull out a chair. 'I heard you arguing with La Roux earlier . . .'

I might as well have *slapped* her, her reaction is so violent. Her head jerks around. She nearly knocks the pan off the cooker. 'And what did you hear?'

'Nothing. Just voices. La Roux said you'd had an argument about the Sharpeville Massacre, which seemed – I don't know – a fairly stupid thing to have an argument about, really.'

Her eyes flash. 'Do you know how many innocent people were murdered at Sharpeville, Medve?'

I shake my head (Am I quite simply the worst person in the world, or am I actually *missing* something here?).

'Sixty-*nine*,' she hisses, 'all unarmed. Peacefully protesting. Women and children.'

'Right,' I inspect my hands. When I look up again, a minute or so later, she seems to have brightened a little. She turns down the stove and walks over. 'Is the plan still on for this afternoon?' she asks.

I rub my cheek. 'I don't know. I was thinking maybe the fun had gone out of it.'

'Oh come *on*,' she whispers (slightly crazy around her edges), 'don't be *ridiculous*. It's going to be fantastic.'

She pulls open a kitchen drawer and stealthily removes a brown paper bag from it. 'I have the thing you wanted here. And I have my front-row seat reserved, upstairs, in the Chaplin Suite, which has a perfect view of the cove.'

164

She yanks out a chair and sits down on it. 'And I've had some ideas,' she says, 'on the very best way to go about it . . .'

Then she cheerfully proceeds to blow on my embers. She huffs and she puffs. She has such a way about her, my little sister, that in five minutes flat, she's completely inflamed me.

Everything else is only *filling*, so I'll cut to the chase. Six p.m. The sun is low. The weather is as good as it needs to be. The coast is clear (Big has taken Feely off on some private mission somewhere. They've been gone for several hours). I get my swimming togs together – my towel, my flip-flops – throw on a bikini. I tie up my hair.

On my way down to the cove I bump into Black Jack with a bee in his bonnet (La Roux's trailing ten steps behind me – in shorts and his balaclava, an eye-boggling combination – and still seems a little mournful after this morning's excitations).

'I was just thinking,' Jack says, 'how it might be fun if we went to see the parliament together. Tomorrow, maybe. The three of us. Or we could invite the others if you think they'd be interested. It's not supposed to be *especially* good this time of year, but it should still be worth seeing . . .'

'Is it far?' I ask quizzically.

'Half an hour. I could borrow a friend's Land Rover. We'd need to time it well, though, to get there for dusk, otherwise you miss all the best of the action.'

La Roux has caught up by now, and brightens visibly at the idea of the starlings. So much so that he invites Jack to come swimming with us. Lucky for me he has some other stuff to do, and slouches off like a big, moribund bullock to slowly get on with it.

165

*Perfect.*

The Mermaid Cove lies at the bottom of a steep, rocky incline. It's circular, slate-bottomed, and ebbs and flows with the sea. To get in there you need to clamber down a badly excavated stone stairway (no safety rope, it's rotted away) which is slippery as hell when it's wet. But as luck would have it, it's dry today.

La Roux loves the cove. He's never ventured here before. He enjoys the cormorants on the cliff-tops, and the tufts of heather and the wild daisies crowned and kissed by frantic spring bees, and the verdant clumps of early clover.

On the way down he finds a huge, hairy caterpillar which he pokes with a twig and then moves off the pathway ('for its own safety', he tells me, solemnly).

Once we reach the bottom I throw down my towel and point to the far end. 'Do you see in the deep section where the water looks paler?' I ask.

He nods. He sees it.

'Well, that's actually a kind of bandstand. It's a huge, flat rock in the water, and Jack told me how, in the old days, in the 1930s when they built the hotel, they sunk the rock there so that during summer parties this tiny band could stand on it and serenade the swimmers and the people on the lawns above, drinking cocktails before dinner. Great idea, huh?'

La Roux likes this notion very much indeed.

'It's a couple of inches under now. I guess the water levels must've risen slightly, over the years.'

'How deep does it get, though,' he asks, 'before you can climb up there?'

'When the tide's starting to go out, like it is now, it can't be more than five and a half foot or so. You could probably make it if you stand on tippy-toe.'

'Okay,' La Roux shrugs, pulling off his balaclava. 'I'm keen to try it if you are.'

He starts wading. The water is cool but it's wonderfully inviting.

(And yes, there's a method to my madness: because of the steep rock walls all around us, if Patch is to clearly witness this tantalizing saga unfolding from the privacy of an upstairs window, I will need to be standing slightly higher than the water level.

'The old bandstand', she explained to me earlier, over the kitchen table, 'will be like an ancient stage on which you'll re-enact your masterful revenge like some kind of exquisitely formal, pre-Oedipal Greek drama.' She seems to simply *love* this idea.)

There are reasons – which for the sake of modesty I can't go into here – why my wade over is not as easy and trouble-free as it might be. But thankfully nothing too disruptive or disastrous happens on the way.

La Roux chatters amiably the whole time (ignoring my distractedness) about how cold the sea is off the Cape coast because of the Antarctic current, and how stormy it can be, and how treacherous, and how fine I look in my bikini (Is he mad? Or blind? Or just too easily pleased to be *human*?).

At one point he even thinks he feels something slippery under his big toe, but then he realizes it's just a stray piece of seaweed.

We reach the rock basically intact. I take my time pulling myself on to it (La Roux chuckles uncontrollably when he

167

espies my bikini bottoms – heavy with water – slipping off my rump, but I rectify this situation immediately). Then I politely give La Roux a hand.

He's in his element. I silently observe how what little remained of his cheek-bite make-up has now been all-but washed away (and this, if anything, strengthens my resolve).

'If 'twere done, Medve,' I counsel myself quietly, ''tis best 'twere done quickly . . .' So while La Roux stands – his hands on his hips in a saucy manner like he thinks he's Sir Edmund Hillary or somebody – looking like a soggy but anaemic ginger stick-insect, I turn my back on him, give a little yell, then start yanking frantically at my bikini knickers.

'What's the matter?' he asks, almost instantly panicked.

I hop about a bit, on one foot, and then on the other.

'What's *wrong*?' he repeats, anxiously surveying my little war-dance. I don't answer him directly. I just pant maniacally and prance around.

'What's *happening*?' he bellows, taking an apprehensive step closer.

'I think . . . I *think*,' I finally stutter, 'I think there's something *horrible* up inside my knickers.'

And that, dear friends, is when I do it. I yank them down to knee-level, I turn around, I bend over, I insert my hand into the approximate, intimate parameters of my vaginal area, and then, from its soggy and protesting confines, I remove a five inch, red-coloured, jelly-textured, thirty-seven-scraggy-legged centipede.

La Roux is *not* a happy-chappie. He gives a yell, and then a scream (I kind of hoped he'd fall backwards, into the water, but instead he slips over and lands flat on his coccyx).

168

I turn, I whoop, I chuck that rubber fucker into the air, I yell, 'You thought you'd got one over on me, you little *shit*, but I *knew* about the capped tooth and the make-up and *everything*!'

La Roux doesn't utter a single word back at me. He just shakes his head, gingerly fingers the waistband of his swimmers and breathes deeply. He's plainly considering *vomiting* as an option.

I glance up, grinning, towards the Chaplin Suite, and do my utmost to squint in through the window. The sun's reflecting quite strongly, so at first I can't see anything, but eventually I'm able to distinguish . . . not Patch.

Not *only* Patch, I mean, but *four* faces. Staring down at me. Big and Patch and *Poodle* and little Feely (presumably balanced on a chair). And Patch's fat face is puce with the gloating satisfaction of her low-down and dirty *scheming* little victory.

I guess, as I stand there, that I'm pretty much up shit creek without a paddle. And, frankly – I suddenly start thinking – panties might actually be a rather useful addition down here.

# 17

The bitch is *back* but with an *Eton Crop* – it's a hairstyle, *stupid* – and tits like torpedoes (I know it's not a particularly *original* assessment, but under the difficult circumstances of her sudden return, how fucking *snappy* do you expect me to be?).

And I fear I've really gone and outdone myself this time. There's no shrugging it off or wriggling out of it; I'm in Double Trouble with a capital D. T.

'It's been a long while coming, Medve,' Big announces ominously, when he finally catches up with me (my hair's still wet. I've not even *changed* yet), 'but your day of reckoning is finally here.'

He's not *angry* or anything, just *disappointed* (oh God, how I hate it when parents pull this manoeuvre). He says I've confused and confounded him, that he thought I knew *better*, and where, oh *where*, he wonders, in cacophonous conclusion, is my natural-born *dignity*?

'Well it's certainly not hidden inside her vagina,' Poodle intervenes, bitchily, from her roost in the far corner, 'because we've all had a pretty good look up *there* today.'

'Oh *shit*!' I gasp back at her, in phoney-teen-retaliatory amazement. 'Perhaps it might've taken some brief refuge in the gaping chasm where your sense of *humour*'s meant to be.'

(She doesn't like this. Nor does he.)

'Learn some manners,' Big snaps.

'But where the fuck *from*?' I ask indignantly.

Oh dear. Three weeks of washing-up duty suddenly lie ahead of me.

*Poodle.* Back again – with no fair warning, either – and the sudden proud possessor of these two *huge* breasts which nobody's allowed to mention under pain of decapitation. But even little Feely seems hypnotized by them. (And he's *never* been a breast man. He was fed by bottle, all the way.)

The same applies to Mr La Roux, who, when he finally meets Poodle face to face (he's been keeping out of harm's way for as long as is decently feasible) acts about as green as a debutante at her coming-out party. He blushes and floor-watches and almost bloody *curtseys*. Well that's sodding *men* for you. Slam-dunked by beauty.

Unfortunately, Poodle seems to have it in for him from the very beginning. The first thing she says after they exchange greetings (and, in fairness, she does actually direct this snide comment towards me) is, 'If I find out who taught Feely that pathetic burping habit I'm going to stitch up their rectum and then feed them molasses.'

(My older sister means business. She's hard as enamel.)

The next thing she says is, 'What the *fuck* is that smell in here?', and after sniffing the air like a beautiful bloodhound barks. 'It's tea tree oil! I'd recognize its rotten, antiseptic scent *anywhere.*'

(Ah, so this solves *that* mystery.)

La Roux and I – as part of my Draconian Punishment Regimen – have now been formally forbidden from spending time together. We are not to be trusted alone under any circumstances, and the only words we are permitted to utter must either be completely uncontentious or absolutely necessary (like *'Fire!'*, or 'Pass the ketchup', or 'I think Feely's hyperventilating', which he does after supper. Too much burping, apparently).

Naturally I corner Patch in the kitchen later that same evening and quietly prepare to kick her head in. But – believe it or not – La Roux (who has ears like a whippet) comes storming on in at an inopportune moment and literally, physically drags me off her.

'Violence is no solution, Medve,' he tells me (thereby violating every punitive penalty I am currently labouring under) 'to this fine mess you've got us into.'

'Wanna *bet*?' I bellow, and then I pause for a second. 'Hang on. Who the hell do you think you *are*? Oliver fucking *Hardy*? The fine mess *who* got us into, anyway?'

He shakes his finger at me. 'I think you probably heard me the first time, young lady.' (Young *lady*? What a *dweeb*.)

And do you think the fat brat is grateful for his muscular intervention? Is she *heck*! Not a jot of it! 'I can fight my own bloody battles,' she yells, then marches off brazenly.

Is it just me, or has Poodle gone and soured *everything*?

When supper is over (a monosyllabic occasion – La Roux and Feely staring, as if hypnotized, at Poodle's sweet-scented and expensively encased bazookas, Poodle wincing at La Roux's eating habits, Big inquiring constantly about Mo and Bob Ranger, Poodle evading him fairly ineffectually . . . 'Yeah, they're working very *hard* together . . .', Patch and me still both sulking competitively: and guess who's *winning*?)

Poodle comes downstairs to help me with the washing-up.

As soon as she thinks everyone is out of earshot, she throws in the towel and pulls out a chair. 'Okay, Medve,' she tells me, 'we've got to get the South African out of here. And I mean yesterday.'

I turn and glare at her. 'Why?'

'It's nothing personal, but his father's sending Mo money and that's the only reason she can currently afford to stay in America. The way I see it, we really need her home again.'

'But I thought she was doing pretty well out there?'

Poodle growls exasperatedly. 'She's *this* fucking close, you moron,' she flashes me an inch gap between her pretty fingers, 'to leaving him.'

I blink. 'Leaving *who*?'

Her huge eyes widen. 'Our poor *father*, stupid! Why the hell else would I decide to come back here? You honestly think I don't have other places I'd much rather be?

'And *anyway*,' she continues, 'Big could get into serious trouble if he's found guilty of giving shelter to an illegal immigrant. He's the last person in the world who needs visa problems at the moment. Something like this could be a major black mark against him . . .'

I think she's exaggerating, but before I can say anything I hear gentle steps on the stairway, so tip my head and *shush* her.

Five seconds later Big appears, and he's beaming.

'I've been speaking to Jack,' he tells us, 'and he was saying he'd had this great idea of taking us as a family to see a parliament of starlings. He's borrowing a friend's Land Rover tomorrow evening. It's a very kind offer. Are the two of you interested?'

Poodle shrugs (she's not much of a nature lover) and I nod.

'Great. Then I'll go and tell him.' He prances off again.

'I still can't believe you got your breasts done,' I snipe, returning to my washing-up duties (still in quite a tizzy about the South African dilemma). 'How much did they cost you? I bet that ancient, leather-faced travel agent put his hand to his pocket.'

'You know what?' she oozes back at me. 'I really can't *believe* you're still growing. Just a couple more months and that huge, fat head of yours will be scraping the ceiling.'

Oh *God*, how I hate her.


Big loves this girl *so* dearly that it is literally *sickening* to watch him around her. She makes him happy. He finds her funny. They go on special little walks together. They talk about the progress he's making in the shrubberies and with his pathetic Yank crochet wall-hanging.

She confides in him about her surgery and how much having it done *meant* to her. And he tells her how he thinks it's the person *inside* that really matters, so in his book she's always been perfect *anyway*.

Can you believe all this clap-trap?

Yeah. So I won't bother denying how hard it is having my beautiful older sister back home again. (I'm feeling like the outcast crow who never receives an invite to the fox's cheese dinner.)

Suddenly, *Poodle*'s the one Feely wants to read him a bedtime story. And Black Jack turns and stares after *her* when she totters past him in her expensive lizardskin heels and flying jacket (like she's a gentle thief who's stolen his eyes away).

Even La Roux. Even *he* jumps on the bandwagon.

Over breakfast (on the morning after her arrival), he asks her courteously whether he can pour her more coffee (yes, we're all drinking coffee now because this is Poodle's brand-new beverage of preference). He's stopped wearing his balaclava. His hair is oiled and shiny. His nails are clean. He's even stopped *smelling*, temporarily.

It's just too much disappointment for a single, ugly, gangly, envious girl giant to handle. So I spend the morning fishing, on my own. Thinking.

I mean, perhaps La Roux *would* be better off leaving. And perhaps Mo *should* come home again. And maybe Barge *is* a talented painter. And perhaps Big *isn't* as small as he seems . . .

And maybe Feely *should* stop burping. And perhaps I really *ought* to start considering acting my age instead of my shoe-size (although the two – strictly speaking – are virtually identical).

Surprise *surprise*. The damn fish aren't biting. I don't catch a thing. But I *do* overhear an extraordinary conversation – on my return home for lunch – strolling through the foyer. Voices from the Ganges Room.

Poodle and La Roux. And she's quietly and calmly asking him to *go*.

'I don't expect you to understand,' she tells him, 'but there are certain personal, family problems which only your leaving can rectify.'

La Roux doesn't speak a word.

'Big could get into trouble if the authorities find out you're here. And the situation with Medve at the moment isn't ideal,

175

either. Anyhow,' she wheedles in that awfully sweet but horribly *direct* way she's perfected to an art form over the years,
'I'm sure there must be people back in South Africa who are
missing you terribly.'

'The thing with Medve,' La Roux intervenes, 'just got a little
out of hand . . .'

Poodle ignores him. 'Big was telling me that you were a
medic in the army,' she slithers, 'which I thought was *wonderful*.'

La Roux is silent again.

'And the point is,' she continues, 'if you really didn't want
to go back for some reason, with the political situation as it is
out there, I'm sure you could say you had *moral* objections to
fighting in the war. Or that you were actively opposed to
apartheid or something. I'm certain they'd buy it if you were
sufficiently convincing . . .'

When La Roux next speaks, it is in a strange, dark voice. 'I
could *never*,' he whispers hoarsely, 'I could *never* do that. It
would be wrong. It would be cowardly. It would be cheap
and weak and *underhand*.'

Oh dear. This is turning nasty. And I'm seriously thinking
about sticking out my small chest and sticking in my big beak,
when I suddenly hear footsteps, behind me, coming my way,
so I turn on my tail and scarper, determining to corner Poodle
later and have my bloody say.

After lunch – a sedate affair in the dining-room, with Poodle presiding – La Roux passes me on the stairs. We're heading in opposite directions. 'I have nowhere else to go,' he
whispers. Then he slowly continues descending, as if he
hasn't even spoken.

*

Patch has quite lost her glow. I don't know how or why exactly, but she's suddenly awfully pale of face and full of lethargy. Later that afternoon, when we're all preparing to head off and see the starlings, she says she feels under the weather and asks to stay at home instead.

La Roux – he's back wearing his balaclava again, which I presume must be a good sign – kindly offers to stay with her, but she shakes her head and mutters how she'd much rather be alone. At which point Poodle steps in and won't take no for an answer.

She pulls off her coat and says she's not particularly interested in seeing a pack of noisy, greasy starlings flying around anyway. So that is *that*, then.

Much as I expected, the starlings are further away than Black Jack anticipated. We drive for fifty minutes, Feely, Big and me crammed on to the front seat, La Roux sitting alone in the open back, his balaclava off, his hair flying in the slipstream, and he's sneaking the odd opportunity – when the impulse takes him – of hanging his head over the side and howling like an uptight, ill-trained, overexcitable puppy.

When we finally reach our location – a strangely flat, isolated and marshy area with extensive reedbeds concealing angry coots who yell from their hidden corners when we first arrive like irritable feathered fire alarms – the sky is grey and dusky. It's also pretty damn *empty*.

Black Jack parks the car and we all clamber out. Nobody says anything. Silence. The odd coot shouts. Silence again. After fifteen minutes Big starts getting impatient. Are we in the right place? Is it the proper season?

'Hang on a minute,' La Roux says, spinning on the spot, 'can't you hear something?'

We all hold our breath and listen. At first I hear nothing. And then, a kind of windy noise, a swishing. *Wings.* Beating.

They've *come.* In their thousands. Like a hurricane. But silent, and ghostly. Not a stray tweet or an angry twitter among them. They arrive like a plague of feathers. Like a glossy, black whirlwind. A tornado of starlings, darting and spinning and turning and spiralling. Making shapes in the sky. Flying in formation. But madly. And randomly.

A million birds. One huge, great organism. One cloud. Then they divide. And join up again. They draw tigers in the air, and steam trains and pythons. They annex the sky in a single, stealthy, inky occupation of rapturous beak and shiny claw and piercing eye. Turning one way, then the other.

I glance at La Roux. He's just to the right of me. His face is turned to the heavens, his mouth is open. He is *crying*.

When the sun has flown and the birds have set, La Roux takes a deep breath, then stands tall and turns and faces the assembled company.

'I thought you should know,' he says, clumsily pulling his balaclava back on again, 'I'm so very grateful for all the things you've done for me, and I'm leaving in the morning.'

Then we drive home, *darkly*.

It's a long night. Jack Henry spends the best part of it scurrying around inside my head catching cockroaches and devouring them 'for the protein'. When he pauses for a moment, he tells me this story about how he once used his regulation Bible to make a club during a long run in solitary – he used water from the lavatory and constructed it out of papier maché – then when one of the guards popped his head in to check up on him, he bludgeoned him soundly with it. Cut him quite badly.

The man had been systematically tormenting him, he tells me, like you are, he says, *like you are*.

He seems to think this story is terribly funny for some reason. But when he laughs his stomach starts hurting. *Bile*. So he stops laughing and quietly starts hunting for bugs again.


I am awoken by Black Jack, banging heavily on the front door, and calling. It's too early. Everything's still dazy. I crawl out of bed to answer him. He's breathless. He's panting. He just got a call from the mainland, he says. Some people from the immigration service have asked for a quick lift over.

'I've got to go,' he tells me. 'I delayed enough already.'

Big's coming downstairs, rubbing his eyes, but I sprint up past him. Top floor, dark corridor, aquamarine door. I burst in.

La Roux is standing by the window. It is five-thirty a.m.

'You've got to get out of here,' I tell him, 'the immigration people are coming. Maybe wait until they're off the tractor and heading up here, then run around the back way and try crossing the water. It won't be too deep. We'll keep them busy in the meantime.'

He doesn't say anything. He doesn't say *anything*.

It's bleak and bad and quiet and grey. It feels like we are dreaming.


The Immigration People, when they arrive, are the Immigration Person. One woman. Called Sandy. Skinny. Polite. Hails

179

originally from Saffron Walden. Owns a pug, called Maudsley, she tells Big pleasantly over a quick cup of tea. A pedigree.

Believe it or not, she's in no particular hurry.

He was never going to make it over. Can't swim. Too risky. And the tide's still strong. They pick him up, later, in a rowing boat. He's wandering around aimlessly, waist-high in the water. The whole thing isn't even scary or frightening. Just sad, and strange and a little embarrassing.

# 18

They tell us to pack the rest of his stuff together. So I go and I do it. The stupid white clay pipe, the cushion cover his mother made him, the picture of Spookie, his army pyjamas. His pony sweater.

On my way downstairs Big calls out my name and scurries up and – almost apologetically – shoves two spare crochet needles and two balls of wool into my hands. Then he scuttles off again.

Downstairs, in the kitchen, Patch is still lying face-down on the pine table, sobbing uncontrollably. Feely is sitting on his bean-bag, just next to her, like a clucky hen, staring up at the ceiling where the fan's revolving.

I'm tearless, at this point, and resolving coldly to stay that way. But then something awful happens. On my way over to the mainland – the sea is gone, the sand is back, the beach is dry – Black Jack comes running down after me.

'If you're seeing him,' he says, panting . . .

'I'm not seeing him. I'm just dropping his stuff off at the Post Office. They're picking it up later.

'Well, anyway . . .'

He puts his hands into his pockets and pulls out three slightly battered packets of Iced Gems, and a fully illustrated colour book of British birdlife. 'I thought he might like these,' he shrugs, 'as something small to remember me by.'

And that's what finally gets me. The tears start welling and before I know it I'm bawling like a baby. And once I start, it's difficult to think about stopping again. Because then, when I do, I know it will all truly be over. And he'll be gone for ever. Back to South Africa. And military prison or wherever the hell they take people like him. And I know I'll never see the skinny, self-centred, stupid, impolitic mother-fucker again.

On my miserable trudge back home to the hotel, I glance up and see Poodle sitting on the wall at the edge of the balcony, swinging her legs and staring blankly out to sea. I walk over and stand in front of her, seething. She smiles down at me, unfocused, almost dreamy. 'I can see Outer Hope quite clearly from here,' she tells me idly, 'it's such a clear day.'

'Christabel,' I snap back at her, my voice as tight as a skinny-rib-sweater, 'I will never, *never* forgive you for the thing you did today.'

And I'm sixteen years old. And my nose is running. But I mean it. And I stand by it. I never will forgive her. Not ever.

She just stares at me impassively. 'I think you should know that Patch is going to have a baby,' she says. Then she glances down the coast again like she finds the view captivating.

That night, when I'm sleeping, a piece of glass falls out of the ceiling. Green glass. And smashes into a thousand pieces next to the safe, warm place where I'm lying and I'm dreaming. But not of Jack Henry. For some strange reason, he's gone away. He's left me.

What more can I say? She was thirteen when she had it. A boy.

She called it Michael. (How uninspired is *that*?) The father was fifteen and lived in Scilly. Mo came back. We moved to Skye. It was cold. It was weird. It was winter. And *dreary*.

But before that, even, on the 18th of July, Jack Henry murdered a man called Richard Adan, a Cuban actor–waiter in a restaurant called the Boni-Bon. New York. Early one summer morning. For no particular reason. Then he went on the run. And they caught him. And they locked him up again.

The book sold. It made him a fortune. And a short while after, a famous comedian contacted him in prison and bought the film rights for a quarter of a million.

A few years later, when I'm a little older, I finally get to see a picture of Jack Henry Abbott. He's not at all as I imagined. He has bouffant hair – this strange and audacious teddy-boy affair – like a pompadour. Jack Henry. A *poseur*. Who would have thought it?

And Patch says, 'I'm sure if I'd seen a picture, I would've felt differently about him way back then . . .'

She's a teenager now. She doesn't know any better. And although I take her point, I'm not really sure if I agree with her . . .

Well, not *entirely*, anyway.


Here's something funny. In 1995 I lose my older sister. She goes on some stupid skiing trip to Austria and ends up dead. At this stage, there's only two of the family remaining in England. That's Patch and me. So we go on a trip to the airport together, along with an undertaker, to collect the body.

And that's when Patch tells me. 'It wasn't Poodle who phoned the immigration people, all those years ago,' she says, staring up at the flight numbers, clutching a Styrofoam cup of coffee. 'It wasn't Poodle who betrayed La Roux, Medve. It was me. It was *me.*'

At first I'm not really listening. I don't know what she's saying. I can't make sense of it.

'Because he knew I was pregnant. But I swore him to secrecy. I thought if no one knew, then it would go away. So I set you both up in the cove that day. I thought Big'd get rid of him, after. But he didn't. So I phoned them. The immigration people. And then later, when she put two and two together, Poodle said she'd pretend it was her. Because you were so *angry*. And I felt so *terrible*. And I was *frightened*.

'She said you hated her anyway, so it wouldn't really matter. But I suppose it did, in the end.'

I'm not looking at Patch. I'm staring up at the flight numbers. It's eleven fifty-nine p.m. and fifty-seven seconds, and the screens are glowing, and my eyes are filling.

'My God,' I mutter, 'did you know it was St Valentine's Day?'

And as soon as I've uttered it, we're in the day after.

*I guess it's time to pull those pins out. I'm getting quite dozy. I don't know if I've been sleeping. But the acupuncturist returns and starts twiddling again. He takes out seven. 'But the single one, in this ear,' he says quietly, 'I'm going to cover with a small plaster and leave there. So whenever you feel the urge you can give it a twirl, and hopefully it'll help you.'*

*He does just as he says. Then I sit up and the bed creaks. He goes to the door. He passes through it, and into the reception area. He writes me out a bill and signs it. He hands it over. I take it.*

*'You know what?' he says casually, as I scrabble in my bag for my*

money. 'I honestly believe you are sick enough and mad enough to walk out of here today without even openly acknowledging to me who the hell you are.'

I find my purse and open it.

'Big spoke to your dad about a year ago. They bumped into each other on holiday in Florida. He said you were here, and I was in England for a while, so he wrote and he told me. '

La Roux shrugs his shoulders, like this is just an everyday occurrence, then asks me cordially about the family.

'But I want to know first how you managed to stay here,' I say.

'I didn't. I came back again in 1993. And I settled in Finchley. Then I moved to Tufnell Park. And I've grown quite attached to it actually.'

'But what about the mousebird,' I ask, frowning, 'and the huge moths and the hail stones and the badly behaved apes near Cape Point who molest the tourists. And what about Grape Fanta?'

He smiles. 'I can get that here now, if I feel the urge, at certain, specialist retailers. And you know what?' he tells me, 'I like British birds. Even though they're kind of dowdy. I still have that book Black Jack sent me. I know the robin and the jay and the wren and the stonechat. I know their songs and their eating habits and their favoured terrain and everything.

'In fact,' he continues, grinning, 'I was actually maid of honour at Black Jack's wedding. He had a better man than me as best man already.'

I blink. 'Black Jack? Somebody actually married him?'

'Two years ago. He met this tiny Maori girl and settled in New Zealand near a place called Rotorua which is full of geysers and the smell of sulphur. And they have a whole theme park there dedicated to the kiwi fruit . . .' He pauses. 'You know, even though they grow

185

it in South Africa, the first time I ever ate it was with you and Patch and Feely . . . Tell me about Feely,' he says.

'Oh God,' I grin, 'he's living in Sydney, Australia. He's a performance artist now. He sets fire to stuffed animals, puts them out by pissing on them, then paints himself with the wet, black ashes. It's all ridiculously dramatic.

'He's in love with a man called Samson who has thirty-seven piercings. They have five miniature Schnausers together. He's only four foot nine, but hugely muscular. He never got the regulation boy-growth-spurt in his mid-teens, which was problematic to begin with, but he eventually got over it.'

'And Poodle?' La Roux asks, still smiling. I pause and swallow.

'She died in 1995. In February. On Valentine's Day. From this crazy little blister she got when she was skiing in Austria. She got blood poisoning and it killed her. It was really stupid. It was just one of those improbable things . . .'

He looks briefly crestfallen. 'Big never mentioned it,' he says, 'in any of his letters.'

'He never talks about it. She was always his favourite.'

'It seems like true beauty is destined to live a short life only,' he says sadly.

For some reason this irritates me. 'Talking of letters . . .' I quickly change the subject, 'I wanted to say thanks for the lovely lace penguin you sent from prison. It was very, very sweet of you.'

(Naturally I don't mention how I still sleep with it, propped up on my pillow, and how I bought some tea tree oil from a New Age pharmacy and doused this scruffy, ill-constructed, flightless bird with it. Or how I smell it at night when I'm dreaming and it fills my head with hospital dramas and minor infections and the horrible prospect of clinical enemas.)

186

He shrugs. 'It's always hard to know what to send for a baby.'

(Oh Jesus. How embarrassing.)

'Michael', I stutter, reddening, 'will be fifteen this year. He collects military medals and has a slow eye. He's a revolting child but a real addition to the family.'

For some reason La Roux seems temporarily awestruck. 'Do you think . . .' he stutters, '. . . she might've actually named him after me?' And his eyes start welling. (Michael? Is he serious?! So is that where it came from?)

'And you, Medve?' he mumbles finally.

So I tell him how I trained to be a solicitor, because of stupid Jack Henry, and how I hated myself for hating him when he betrayed us all so badly, and how I married a Grand Larcenist called Jordan while I was practising in America. And how it lasted for six months and then we wanted to kill each other (He likes this bit especially. He's still a little shit, when it finally comes down to it).

And then I tell him how Big is living in Acapulco, with his second wife who's a dietician. How he still lives on soya and has a beard to his breastbone. And how Mo married Bob Ranger in the end, but they were never really very happy, but how the Probe might finally be becoming a viable proposition, fifteen years later (God, who would have thought it?), and how she's writing a definitive text about the coil which is due for publication next February (but only in non-Catholic countries).

'The coil?' La Roux asks, dumbly.

'A form of contraception popular in the seventies,' I tell him.

'Oh.'

And then the conversation fizzles out, and to avoid resorting to talking about the weather and how he's losing his hair a little, and how his sideburns are preposterous, I make a fuss about settling the *bill and how much better I feel already with the pin in my lobe and all the rest of that crap. Then his three-thirty appointment arrives, a woman with a limp like a Grand National faller.*

*And then it's time I was going. And I say goodbye. And I leave him. And it's over. It's all finally over. And I walk down the street, swinging my arms and congratulating myself on what a good plan it was to see him, and how well it went and everything. How glad I was I didn't mention that it was Patch who turned him in, not Poodle. How glad I was I didn't still blame him for making me hate my bigger sister and how she went and died so inconsiderately without me ever getting around to forgiving her. Or her forgiving me.*

*I walk into the station. I feed my ticket into the machine and retrieve it when it spits it out again. I walk down onto the platform. I push my hand into my bag and pull out some notes on a case I'm thinking about taking. A man who killed a neighbour's cockerel because it woke him every morning at three a.m.*

*I've learned something, I keep telling myself (but I don't know what it is, and I don't know if I care). I tap my foot. I inspect my watch. The platform fills up, gradually. The station master makes an announcement that there's five more minutes until the train arrives. Because someone went under at Mile End. Again. Poor fucker.*

*I look down at my notes. I think I'm really concentrating. Then there's some kind of commotion at the end of the platform. I keep on reading. The cockerel was called Jasper and it lived in a kennel.*

*The yelling continues. It's something indecipherable. I notice that I'm frowning because suddenly I'm not concentrating. The voice is getting louder still.*

*'The girl penis!' it's shouting. 'Do you remember? The girl penis! It changed my fucking life. I forgot to tell you. I needed to tell you.'*

*He stands, out of breath, next to me on the platform. And every-*

body's frowning because he's a South African.

'I just wanted to tell you,' he gasps, 'about the girl penis and how it changed everything. It was a revelation.'

He collapses on to a bench, his skinny legs sticking out at all angles. 'And I've got something,' he pants cheerily, 'that I wanted to show you.'

He pulls it out of his pocket. His face is glistening. I sit down next to him, cautiously. He opens his hand and shows me. A small, red, plastic centipede, browning with age.

'My God, you kept it?'

He nods. 'Fished it up from the bottom of the cove. Took me almost two hours.'

He shrugs apologetically, as if he doesn't want me to make too much of it. 'I'm such a hoarder, I'd hoard my own arse if it wasn't already attached to me.'

He leans away and inspects my profile. 'You know, I've missed that chin,' he says, 'and I'm glad you've remained as implausibly tall as ever.'

Then he takes a deep breath and slaps his knees and makes as if he's readying himself to leave again. 'I've got someone waiting,' he confides, 'back at the surgery with one of the worst arthritic heels I've ever yet had the privilege of encountering.' (The thought seems to excite him enormously.)

'My train's just coming, anyway,' I tell him, pointing aimlessly towards the tunnel. 'And I've got work to do.'

He raises an imperious ginger eyebrow. I show him the case notes. 'I'm thinking of defending some guy who murdered a cockerel called Jason which lived in a kennel and crowed every morning at three a.m.'

La Roux scowls.

'Oh fuck,' I say. 'You love hens. I forgot. Sorry.'

189

*I put the papers away as he stands up and distractedly unfastens his white overall and reveals one of the most offensive tie-dye sweaters I've ever yet laid eyes upon (in all of my hideously multifarious hippie incarnations).*

*'Well, Medve,' he smiles ingratiatingly, 'I certainly hope you're well on your way to giving up that demon weed.'*

*He holds out his hand as if he wants to shake mine. I do the same. We shake. We let go again.*

*'If you must know, I don't actually smoke,' I mutter.*

*'That's good then,' he mutters back, 'because I'm not really an acupuncturist.' He shrugs. 'I trained as a tailor.'*

*'You're kidding me?'*

*'Of course I am, stupid,' and then he starts chuckling in that maddeningly flat, South African way I well remember from years ago. 'My Lord,' he sniggers, 'I could always play you like a fiddle.'*

*In fact, he finds the whole thing so amusing he even slaps his bony thigh. I peek in his mouth as he's laughing. He's still got terrible teeth, I tell myself, just as bad as I remember. And he still stinks of tea tree. And his skin is still awful. And as if things weren't bad enough already, he seems to have started wearing the worst kind of thick, yellow, plastic-soled, all-animal-product-free shoes with huge silver buckles.*

*I bet, I think to myself, he's become a vegetarian, and that he makes the whole world suffer for it. And, you know, it kind of makes me like him even better. But I tell myself it doesn't.*

*He leans against the wall and we're both quiet for a while. I'm waiting for something, but I don't know what. Then I hear the train coming from deep down in the tunnel. I push my heels together and I pick up my bag, and I firm my resolve. It's time I was going.*

*'Still play a mean game of ping-pong?' La Roux asks casually, over the increasing racket. But soon the roar is too loud for me to say*

190

*anything, and my stupid hair blows everywhere, and the brakes squeak, and the doors swish open. And everybody clambers off. And then everybody else clambers on again.*

*And still,* still *– for some utterly inexplicable reason – I'm sitting on the bench and he's leaning against the wall. And the doors shut. And the train leaves. And the seconds slowly tick by in a glorious infinity as we both quietly wait and idly wonder what my final answer will be.*